ALIEN JEOPARDY

MATED & AFRAID
BOOK 1

JANUARY BELL

ALIEN JEOPARDY

Cover Illustration by @isa.sketches

Typography by Alison Milsap

Published by January Bell

www.januarybellromance.com

Edited by Happy Ever Author

Copyright © 2025 January Bell

This is a work of fiction. Unless otherwise indicated, all the names, characters, businesses, places, events and incidents in this book are either the product of the author's imagination or used in a fictitious manner. Any resemblance to actual persons, living or dead, or actual events is purely coincidental.

All rights reserved. No portion of this book may be reproduced in any form without permission from the publisher, except as permitted by U.S. copyright law. For permissions contact: admin@januarybellromance.com

For sub-rights inquiries, please contact Jessica Watterson at Sandra Djikstra Literary Agency.

❦ Created with Vellum

AUTHOR'S NOTE

For a full list of content notes please visit www.januarybellromance.com.

CHAPTER ONE

ELLISON

IF I GRIT my teeth any harder, I'm going to have to start wearing my stupid nightguard during the day.

Which would just make it a plain old retainer. Just livin' the thirty-three-year-old teenage dream.

I stare at the clock at the bottom of the screen, wishing it would tick by faster.

Twenty-six minutes.

Twenty-six minutes until this pointless meeting that could have been an email is over and I can finally drag my ass out of this uncomfortable chair and do something less brain-meltingly boring.

A text dings through, popping up on my laptop screen.

> Lily: I'm bringing so much tequila

Notification: Lily has changed the group name from Reality Hussies to Drunk To Escape Reality Hussies

> Poppy: ha
>
> Poppy: I'm making brownies right now
>
> Poppy: And I have a crockpot with queso going

My stomach growls in anticipation.

> Ellison: I'll pick order some tacos from that place by my house
>
> Lily: I can't wait
>
> Lily: Lucy, what are you bringing
>
> Lu: My blender for your tequila. Margaritas?
>
> Lu: That okay with you, Ell?

I drag my gaze away from the nonstop notifications coming through my laptop long enough to realize everyone on my stupid video call is quiet.

"Good to hear. I don't see a problem there. Any reports from your team, Trent?" I ask, pretending like I've been listening.

I don't have to listen.

I wrote the damn agenda, because my boss can't be bothered to do shit besides say things like "put a pin in it and circle back" or "team synergy is important" or "can you get me a coffee?"

I hate this job. I click around, waiting for Trent to respond, hoping like hell my fave fanfic author has posted a new chapter in the five minutes since I last checked.

"My team is worried about the current workflow but anticipates—" he starts.

I immediately tune him out.

No new updates on the Suevan fanfic, sadly. I put myself back on mute and tap out a quick response to the group while smiling vaguely at the camera, making just enough eye contact to sell the lie that I'm listening.

It's truly one of the few things this job's taught me to do well: pretending to listen while I think about anything but insurance underwriting.

I'm a true thespian, really.

It's the only field I could find work in since graduating college in post-Roth-invasion Earth. It sucks, but it's money, even though the money doesn't get close to making up for the fact that I'm absolutely bombarded with the fact our planet's gone to shit since the Roth invaded and it's only getting worse.

Familiar dread makes a knot in my stomach, and I exhale slowly, trying to harness some of my hard-won peace.

> Ellison: That sounds so freaking good. I'll have the usual stuff, but tacos and margs and binge watching WME sounds like an ideal night

World's Most Eligible, or WME, is the biggest reality

TV show right now, and me and my tight group of friends are hardcore addicts of it and all reality TV shows.

From the ones where they have to survive on the side of a volcano for a month to the ones where they're ice-fishing and falling in love, to WME, the most absurd dating show I've ever witnessed, we're in.

> Poppy: I've been dreaming about candy all week
>
> Lily: I've been dreaming about getting shit-faced all day
>
> Ell: You might have a problem, Lily
>
> Lily: Yeah, my problem is that life sucks and it feels like the world's going to end any minute

I grimace, glancing back at Trent, who's still droning on about whatever currently is making him feel important. What would he do if he couldn't put a pin in it?

Where, exactly, is he putting that pin?

I'm not sure I want to know.

The alarm on the bottom of the video software blinks, signaling our allotted conference time is up, and I lean back, exulting in the passage of time.

"Alright, everyone, I'm sorry to interrupt, but please send any final thoughts to the group e-mail. Trent, thank you for volunteering to put together call notes for us today," I chirp.

Trent nods officiously, and I resist the urge to flip off

my camera and tell my coworkers that I hate this job and go out in a blaze of fire.

But I smile vaguely instead.

"Have a great weekend, everyone. We'll circle back on Monday."

"Bye," I manage, trying my very hardest not to roll my eyes at Trent. I'm pretty sure this meeting would have resulted in a Trent Business Lingo Bingo Blackout, had I been tracking it.

I don't wait for anyone to ask questions, or even respond, so past giving a fuck that I simply exit out of the video conference and slump in my chair.

> Ellison: You know, Lily, tequila might just be the answer tonight

Poppy: Oh, babe, we gotta find you something else for work

Lu: The job market's shit, the Earth is hotter every day

Lily: Meanwhile, the dating pool is ice cold and shit at the same time

I huff a laugh at that. The only dating any of us like is the kind where we live vicariously through starry-eyed singles forced together on a remote island.

Lu: If the fucking Suevans had openings for more wives, I'd probably take them up on it

Poppy: God, they're so hot, right

> Lily: at this point, I'd take a Roth over a human man
>
> Lily: at least they're hot
>
> Lily: heh get it get it

My nose wrinkles.

> Ellison: I'm not into getting burned alive
>
> Ellison: I have to finish up a few things and then you all can start heading over in maybe thirty minutes or so

The girls all respond excitedly, and I grin at the influx of messages I actually want to see before closing the old laptop trying to burn a hole through my thighs.

The things I have to finish up consist of making my tiny apartment look like a normal, functioning human lives here and not a hot mess of a hobgoblin.

And put something on my lower half that's not covered in last night's dinner stains.

I lift an arm, sniffing experimentally at my pit.

I need a shower.

> Lily: Also we're staying the night at your place
>
> Lily: For safety
>
> Poppy: PAJAMA PARTY

Poppy is relentlessly fashionable, an absolute bubble of style and optimism at all times. Compared to my general apathy and pessimism, she's practically radioactively positive. I have a feeling even her idea for party worthy pajamas will be glamorous to the nth degree.

> Ellison: Only if everyone else wants to do that

Lu: I'm in

Lily: One less thing to do after tequila. It's a yes

Lily: You're outnumbered, Ell

> Ellison: I get the first margarita, then

Poppy: Deal

I'm pretty sure I have a cute set of shortie pjs around here. I bought them when I was last dating someone seriously and never wore them again.

Sighing, I stand up. My hips and knees pop at the same time, a clear sign I've been sitting for way, way too long.

Time to clean… both my apartment and—I sniff my armpit—myself.

We're all only half watching the drama unfold on my TV screen. Likewise, the sixth pitcher of frozen margarita is only half full.

I close one eye, squinting at where it wavers on my newly cleaned coffee table. Well, now there's tortilla chip crumbs dusting the surface and some congealed queso keeping it company, along with a few random Swedish Fish swimming towards the cheese blobs.

Might be six pitchers of Lily-made margaritas were way too many.

Or, based on the floaty way I feel, just the exact right amount.

Ha.

"Look, look, lookity look," Poppy screams.

"Fucking hell, Poppy," Lily says, wincing. "We're all right hereeee, you don't... don't have to yell. It'sss too loud."

It comes out garbled, and I snort in spite of myself.

Lucy tips back her head and cackles, some of her margarita sloshing over the rim of her glass. No salt, because we forewent that task after pitcher number two.

Shit. We are all really drunk.

"I'm glad you all are staying the night," I try to say.

It comes out more like *I'mglaaaaddyallrestayinniiiight.*

"Ell is shitfaced," Lily announces, like a proud new parent.

I close one eye, then the other, trying to bring her into focus.

Poppy stamps her adorable little kitten heel on the floor. Yes, kitten heel, complete with a tuft of fur or feathers or something soft-looking on the strap across her foot. They match her sexy little slip perfectly, and she looks adorable and stylish as usual.

I curl my lip as I pluck at my Hawaiian-print shorts. "At least I'm comfy," I tell myself.

Poppy jabs a finger into my shoulder.

"We're doing this," she says, and I sway a little at the impact of her fingertip.

"Doing what?" Lily asks, always game. That's Lily for you, though.

"I found a reality show that need contestants," Poppy says breathlessly.

Then she hiccups, and we all laugh way too loud and too long.

"It better not be a survival one. You know we'd be the first kicked out," Lucy says, somewhat coherently.

"Speak for yourself," I slur. "I won best archer at camp. I am great with a bow and arrow."

"When you were tweeeeeelve," Lucy argues.

"You literalllllyyyyy bring that up every time you drink." Lily rolls her eyes. "Pathetic."

On screen, the current *World's Most Eligible* couple are making out, and I throw a Swedish Fish at the screen. It bounces off and plops into the quickly defrosting frozen margarita pitcher.

"Going for a swiiiiiim," Lucy sings out. "Little fishies in the seaaaa!"

"Shhhhhh," Poppy presses her finger to her lips, staring us all down. "This important. Isss important." She stomps her foot again, and the fur on her heel wobbles dramatically.

"You look hot," I tell her.

"Super hot," Lily confirms, raising her glass so we can cheers.

We miss, and more margarita spills onto the carpet where we've ended up.

It only makes us laugh more, especially when Lily scoops some off the ground to plop in her mouth.

"That is sick," I tell her.

"Five second rule," Lu says.

"Alcohol kills everything," Lily says after swallowing.

I shake my head. I don't think that's quite true, but I can't remember why.

"I'm going to fucking lose it," Poppy says, and tears spring to her eyes. "Listen to me."

"Shit," Lu says, glancing at her. "Everybody shut up. Poppy has to talk. Poppy talk. Poppy cock."

I snort, then regret it as some frozen margarita starts to go up my nose.

I don't even remember taking a sip.

"I'm signing us all up. For this show." Poppy turns her phone screen so we can see it.

"Okay," I shrug. "Why not?"

"What kind of show?" Lu asks.

Poppy squints at her, trying to figure out what her slur meant.

"We've applied a gazillion times and never gotten in," Lily says with a shrug. Her dark brunette bob grazes her shoulder, and she's so pretty it would make me sick if she weren't my friend.

"You're all so pretty," I tell them.

"Focus." Poppy bellows the world, a drunken nightie-clad drill sergeant. "It's a combination adventure and survival," her tongue trips over the words, and she clears her throat.

"Sotally tober," I tell Lu.

Lucy nods knowingly. She tries to wink at all of us, but only succeeds in blinking very slowly.

"Combination adventure and survival—" Lily starts.

"And dating!" Poppy interrupts, holding a finger up.

"Fuck it," I say, holding my now empty margarita glass up to cheers the girls. Half clink against mine, and then we're refilling our glasses.

"Okay, good," Poppy says, slightly breathless. "When?"

"Do they have an ASAP option?" I ask on a laugh. The idea of getting out of my life even for a little bit sounds amazing. Getting to do one of the shows I've been obsessed with since I was a kid with my best friends sounds even better.

"They do," Poppy confirms. "Here. I have a tab filled out for everyone separately. Just pass it around and fill in your socials and sign electronically." She beams at us.

It takes us all way longer than it should, between trips to the bathroom to pee, making another pitcher of margaritas, and forgetting how to spell my last name.

But we get it done.

And before we've drunk our seventh pitcher of frozen margaritas, we're all signed up for the reality TV show Poppy found.

Somewhere between the start and finish of the eighth pitcher, the couple on TV are breaking up for other singles, Poppy's tapping away furiously at her phone, and the rest of my friends are passed out.

Lucy's snores are impressive and alarming, to be honest. I yawn, half-asleep myself.

So when blue light streams through my apartment window, the TV blinking on and off and Poppy standing up on wobbly drunk legs—in her heels—I'm pretty sure I'm dreaming.

Because there's no way I'm really seeing what looks like a spaceship.

That would be silly.

CHAPTER
TWO

KA-REXSH

It's too good to be true.

Surely, there is a trap here somewhere.

I glance around at the four other Draegon males, but if they're worried about this joint-species initiative, they don't show it.

Standing straighter, I flex my wings, running a hand over a horn.

I recognize only one of them — Pol.

He doesn't look worried, but he does look furious.

I can't say I blame him. As the son of our tyrant king, he has every reason to want a fresh start at life.

Which is why all five of us are here.

This is supposed to be our chance to get off planet.

According to the Roth who have planned this, we will provide entertainment for humans, Roth and Suevans alike, and as a reward for finishing this… entertainment, we will receive a parcel of land and a home on Sueva.

And a mate.

A mate.

My cock grows hard, starting to skith at the very thought of a female to call my own. To cherish. My fangs press into my lower lip, but the sting of them doesn't do a thing to damper my enthusiasm at the idea of a mate.

My mate.

It's not the reason I signed up.

No. I wanted off the planet ruled by Pol's father.

I wanted a new chance at a life, where I can do what I want.

But now that I'm here?

I can't stop thinking about what a mate might be like. What she might look like.

The Roth organizer walks into the room where we've assembled, a serious expression on his velvety grey face. The ship we're on is the antithesis of Draegon space cruisers, all sleek chrome and minimalist style.

Draegon prefer everything to be as luxurious and over-the-top as possible. The more gold and gems the better.

Not that I've ever been able to afford more than enough to feed myself.

Still, it's a ship, and it holds the key to my future.

At least, that's what I'm telling myself.

"Your mates have arrived," he says. His nose twitches, and my eyes narrow at the small tell.

"What's wrong with them?" Pol asks the question

before I have a chance to, a growl in his voice. "What tricks are up your sleeve, Roth?"

"They appear to be... inebriated." The Roth shifts his weight, anticipating our anger.

Draegon are not known for our patience and understanding.

Our wings tense as a group, and I share a furious glance with the male standing next to me.

The Roth steps back at the looks on our faces, holding his hands up.

"Don't worry, their paperwork is completely in order, they selected the option for immediate filming, and despite their intoxication, they are all in good health and are excellent candidates for the five of you." He licks his lips. "So we'll simply continue as planned."

"Give them something for their current state," I snarl, angry at the mere idea of my future mate being inebriated when we first meet.

The idea of my future mate without full control of her faculties around the Roth makes my skin crawl, and I rub the spot where my horns grow from my forehead, my tail slashing behind me.

The rest of the males nod in agreement.

The Roth organizer takes another step back. "Of course, we already did. It might take longer because of their delicate human constitution, but they've been seen to. It wouldn't do to have them at a disadvantage so early in the game."

He clears his throat and, slightly appeased, we all glance sidelong at each other.

I could like these males, I decide.

They at least have some honor.

To my right, Pol paces back and forth, agitated enough that his skin's shifting colors, another sign of his royal blood.

It's strange that he's here at all, and I doubt that he's here by choice.

No, if I had to bet, I would say that this is some stunt done by the king to get Pol away from our planet once more.

"The women are behind this glass," the Roth says, and we surge towards him as one, clearly all impatient to get to our mates.

A mate.

I squeeze my eyes shut, the kith of my cock moving so rapidly now that it's nearly painful with need.

"I'll turn the transparency on so you can see them and you'll take turns selecting a mate."

My hands fist at my sides, my talons driving into the flesh of my palm. The slight pain relieves a small bit of the mating frenzy that's started to grip me. Heat rises from the base of my spine, up between my shoulders, to where my wings begin.

My lip curls as a snarl starts to climb from my throat, the mating heat drawing up, up and through the bones of my wings.

It's begun, my body starting the process that will cause the poison of my mate bond to seep from my talon-tipped wings.

I don't bother glancing at the other contestants for this

game we've agreed to play, and I can tell from the tension ratcheting up in the room that we're all solely focused on the women that will be presented to us.

Our mates.

My throat goes dry, and a growl escapes me before I can swallow it.

A tentative smirk plays along the Roth's dark grey lips, and then he taps the opaque surface behind him, turning it transparent—for us, at least. The women seem unaware that we're watching them.

The sight behind the glass nearly brings me to my knees.

Five human women, all scandalously clad, all beautiful in their own way, from plump and curvy to lean and muscled, short to tall.

Only one grabs my attention and holds it.

Reddish brown hair, rumpled and waved, falling around a lovely oval-shaped face, dark lashes framing brown eyes, a dusting of light spots across the bridge of her very human nose.

Rose-red lips part, and the breath's knocked from me at the sight of a pink tongue before a hand covers her mouth, her eyes closing.

The woman on the other side of her elbows her, and I grit my teeth at the contact because no one touches what's mine.

No one.

"I will pick first," Pol announces, and the four of us all make noises of disgust, noises that quickly fall silent as the predatory alpha gaze he flings at us works immediately.

If he picks the woman that's mine, I will kill him.

I roll my shoulders, my feral nature somewhat satisfied by that decision.

"We have assigned you each a number, actually—" The Roth's words are interrupted by Pol stepping close to him, so close that the grey Roth visibly pales.

Interesting. I didn't know their species was capable of that.

"Unless you want me to unleash my fire on you, Roth, you will let your betters decide."

A laugh, unhinged, spills from the purple-skinned Draegon in the back of the room. He's old, much older than the rest of us, his silver hair and ice-blue eyes full of malice.

"Careful there, princeling," he says, the words a sarcastic purr that sets my teeth on edge.

The Roth's throat bobs as we all glance to him, wondering what he'll do.

If he refuses the prince, he may not leave this room alive.

If he doesn't refuse the prince, all five of us may be driven to fight, our instincts screaming to get to the females in the next room.

If the prince picks my woman, I will sate my thirst for blood before he has time to blink.

"Perhaps the females should be allowed to pick," the Roth says nervously.

My tail slashes the air, the idea of my female choosing another male making my stomach churn.

The prince, Pol, glances back at the silver-haired Draegon in the back, then nods.

"That will suffice," Pol announces.

My talons bite further into my skin, and I force my hands to relax at my sides.

She won't pick one of the others.

She can't.

The petite human with the pale skin and spots on her cheeks, with the perfectly thick thighs and careless yawns…

She is the one for me.

My mate.

CHAPTER
THREE

ELLISON

"We aren't dreaming, this isn't a dream," Lucy chants, her usually perfectly tamed blue-black hair a total mop around her head. Dark circles stand out under her eyes.

A speaker crackles, and I make myself stop yawning and stand up a bit straighter.

"Margaritas were a bad choice," Lily mutters, and I nod fervently.

"Welcome to the first season of the brand-new reality show that is sure to be hit," a computerized voice says over the speaker.

"Oh god, we did do that, didn't we," Lu squeaks. She attempts to rake her hand through her thick hair, but her fingers get stuck.

A few tugs and she gives up, several black strands falling to the floor.

A new reality show.

"Poppy," I say slowly, turning to look at my lingerie-clad friend.

She's wringing her hands, her eyes darting around the room like she'd rather look anywhere but at me.

"What day is it?" Lily asks. Her short dark brown hair is messier than usual, and she looks more hungover than anyone else.

"How is this possible?" I ask everyone and no one all at once.

The memory of a blue light in my window flashes through my mind.

The flickering TV screen.

Poppy tapping into her phone.

"Poppy," I grit out.

"At least you don't have to go to work today," she says in a faux bright voice. "You hated that job. Right? We're all living the dream!"

"Poppy," Lu and Lily say together.

"You signed the paperwork. It's not my fault if you didn't read the whole contract through." She sniffs, red blotches of color climbing from her huge boobs up her throat and to her face.

"You knew," I gasp. "You knew that they would get us right away, and you wore lingerie for it." I point at her.

Our friends also gasp, which would be more satisfying if it weren't for the fact that we've definitely been abducted by aliens.

To star on an *alien* reality TV show.

Poppy tosses her perfectly waved auburn hair behind

her shoulder and juts out her chin. "You all have been fucking miserable for ages. I just chose to do something about it."

The four of us all seem to inhale as one, but the computerized voice coming from nowhere and everywhere all at once starts back up.

"You will each be paired with a partner of your choosing to complete the course with. The object is to survive together as you make it to a series of waypoints. At each waypoint, there will be a challenge to complete for a reward that will make your path easier. Each pair will be dropped at a different location on Hylorr, one of the uninhabited moons in the outer rim of the Suevan system. You will be filmed at all times by drones, so as not to disrupt the reality element of the show. Of course, if you get into trouble, you can always quit, but that means that neither you nor your partner will receive the reward."

My eyes widen slightly, because damn it, I'm nothing if not competitive.

And damn me if I don't love a reward. I've been a trophy hound since I was little, when I did gymnastics competitively, always hoping to make it to the Olympics. Of course, they don't hold that contest anymore, and my dreams of gymnastic superstardom went up in flames along with most of the world after the Roth invaded.

Now I'm lucky if I have time or motivation to even work out.

The other four seem just as spellbound by the voice as

I am, and I wonder if we'll be allowed to pair up with each other.

No way am I picking Miss Fur Heels and Negligee, though.

Ugh.

"Suevan system," Lucy finally says, glaring openly at Poppy. "It all makes sense now."

Lily groans and pinches the bridge of her nose. "Poppy, I am officially pissed off at you."

Poppy goes rigid, staring straight at the opaque glass in front of all of us.

I wrap my arms around my chest, annoyed at the fact that not only did she not tell us what we were signing up for, but she didn't think we would agree to it without being wasted.

"You needed a push," Poppy mutters.

My eyebrows skyrocket.

We all turn on our sassy, unapologetic friend at once, but whatever we're going to yell at her stops as the computerized voice starts again.

"The reward is spectacular," the voice booms out, whatever computer is handling this speech attempting to sound even more excited. "Each couple to complete the course successfully will be rewarded with a mansion and a parcel of land on Sueva, as well as one million galactic credits."

"Credits?" Lu whispers, her eyebrows drawn. "That could be like one dollar."

Lily's already raising her hand, and in spite of the situation, I snort a laugh.

"How much money is that in, er, American dollars?" she asks.

There's no answer.

I roll my eyes, catching a small grin on Lu's face.

We might all be pissed off, but none of us are truly angry. Lily looks madder than the rest, but I know the sound of the reward's already put her at ease.

"Before we begin, we have one last contestant to announce." A door slides open with a pneumatic hiss, and a thin, hard-looking woman walks in. Her eyes are dark, her collarbones jutting out sharply from beneath the simple shift dress she wears. Shoulders hunched, she surveys us with suspicious eyes.

"Introducing Selene!"

I nod at her, managing a quiet hello, completely unsure what to think about the newcomer. The rest of my friends look slightly nervous, all greeting her with varied degrees of enthusiasm.

"Why is it just the six of us? That doesn't seem like enough people—" Lucy starts.

"You will be allowed to select your mate now, and once chosen, you will be marked and dropped at a secret location. Good luck to all of you, and welcome to *Mated and Afraid*."

Music starts, dramatic and ridiculous.

"Is that supposed to be the theme song?" Lily asks, frowning. "It's not very good."

Lu laughs at that, then winces. "I'm still so hungover."

"How the hell did they get us to Sueva so fast—"

Poppy gasps, interrupting Lily as she takes several steps forward.

Reflexively, we all look towards where Poppy's heading.

The glass isn't opaque any longer.

Nope.

It's clear, and I swallow hard, my heart beating incredibly fast at the sight on the other side of it.

Five winged aliens, in colors I didn't know aliens came in. Sure, one's green, like the Suevans, and though they have a pattern to their skin, they aren't scaled like the Suevans, or the grey velvet of the Roth. None of them are wearing anything but sturdy-looking pants, weapons strapped to their thighs and hips.

I fan my face.

They're huge.

Huge, and more muscled than anyone I've ever seen in my entire life. Whew.

"Those are our partners?" Lucy sounds like she might faint.

Lily and I share a concerned look. If the opening of this show is anything like the human reality survival shows we like, Lucy and her hangover are in serious trouble.

"You have thirty seconds to choose a partner. Ellison Price, you will choose first."

Oh shit, that's me.

Thirty seconds?

Sure enough, a lit-up clock appears in the glass, ticking down from thirty.

I shake my head, my gaze skimming across the veritable buffet of stunning specimens in front of me. All five seem incredibly tense, their wings all at half-mast, tails flicking like an angry cat's behind them.

Except for one.

He smiles at me, gently, as if he sees how scared and unprepared the four—er, five—of us are. A minty sage green, his strange skin is a refreshing color against the vivid and aggressive shades of oranges and reds and purples. Stripes start on the sides of his chest and stomach, growing darker as they travel towards his back.

I've always been a face card kind of girl, and his is immaculate, if strange. Not that there's anything to complain about when it comes to his body.

A strong jaw, more angular than any I've ever seen, fangs, not dissimilar to the Suevans Poppy's so fond of, golden eyes and thick brows.

Horns seem to sprout from his forehead, arcing over and away from his dark, thick hair. It's tied half up into a bun, and there's something wildly approachable about that despite the male's size and, well, alien-ness.

Not sure that's a word, but last night's tequila does not a poet make.

"Choose," a voice intones, the clock down to five seconds. I point immediately, because I've only really looked at him.

His smile deepens, and something like desire heats my blood.

"The green one," I say.

"Step through and claim your mate," the announcer says, and the alien doesn't hesitate. What I thought was glass ripples like water as the winged green alien steps through it.

"On your mark," the voice continues, and an X glows bright red in front of me.

I step on it, assuming this is some kind of camera-work stage-direction-type thing.

"Good grief," I say, because the moment I look up, the green alien's all but on top of me. "You're huge."

The alien says something I don't understand, and disappointment fills me, followed by anxiety.

We don't speak the same language. My heart pounds against my rib cage, adrenaline and anxiety mixing up and sending my pulse racing.

How are we supposed to win if we can't even communicate?

Shit.

The alien's wings go around me, and I flinch as the tips of them scrape the backs of both my thighs.

"Get set," the voice says.

I scream as the floor opens up, swallowing us whole.

I throw myself at the huge alien in front of me, at a total loss for anything else to do as we freefall through the floor.

"They forgot to say go!" I yell, the words lost to the wind, not that he would have understood them anyway.

His arms wrap around me, holding my weight effortlessly, all while I scream like a wet cat.

Something else wraps around me too, and I kick my

leg, panicking completely, trying to get it off before I realize it's his tail.

He's murmuring to me in a soft, steady stream, and though I don't understand a single fucking word he's saying, I know he's trying to comfort me.

Unfortunately for both of us, we're still falling, and I don't exactly relish the idea of splatting onto a random moon's surface.

No sooner has the word 'splat' gone across my mind than his wings snap open.

I whimper, burying my face into his chest, and trying to breathe as we sail upward.

His tail strokes my calf in some sort of attempt at comfort.

Instinctively, I wrap my legs around his waist as best I can. Not an easy thing to do, considering the freaking size of him.

He groans, and I freeze.

Did I imagine that noise?

I almost convince myself to forget about it, considering we're flying in the air together and I have bigger problems to worry about.

Until he bends his head down, nuzzling the juncture between my neck and shoulder, and inhales.

CHAPTER FOUR

KA-REXSH

My mate.

My female.

My woman.

I inhale her, nostrils flaring, the delicious musk of her skin the most perfect thing I've ever smelled in my entire fucking life. Everything about her is perfect. And she chose me.

She chose me.

Pride fills me, and I beat my wings twice, unable to stop the giddy impulse.

I open my eyes, lifting my head and taking my time staring at her as I fly us towards the drop point they assigned me this morning.

Humans are not unusual on my planet, though the practice of abducting them waned over the centuries.

Still, I've never been this close to one, and I certainly never thought I would be fortunate enough to be mated to one. Only the richest and most powerful of the Draegon could boast mating with one, and human females have been scarce on our planet since the virus that wiped out most of our species' females made them an even more precious commodity.

They are supposed to be able to give pleasure unlike anything our females are capable of, and even now, my cock strains to get to her, to find the valleys and hills of her pleasure and chart a course to her heart.

Having her in my arms is more than I've ever dared hope for.

Already, I can feel her blood heating from the mating poison working its way through her bloodstream.

Deep satisfaction makes my tail tighten where it's wrapped around her thigh. Already, her scent begins to mix with mine.

I am well-pleased.

What better way to learn what pleases her than to complete this contest together? We finish, we receive a place to live on Sueva, a safe home for my mate and land. Nothing could be better.

I could finally be the kind of male that deserves a mate.

A bird of some sort squawks as it nearly glides into me, changing course at the last minute to avoid the collision.

A laugh climbs out of my throat, the sound unfamiliar. When was the last time I truly laughed?

When was the last time I felt as free as I do now, flying across the alien moon with my female in my arms?

Never.

I am certain I have never felt as free, as complete, as I do with this soft woman melting against my body.

CHAPTER
FIVE

ELLISON

We are flying.

Flying.

All of my irritation with Poppy has drained away thanks to my brain catching up with the sheer impossibility of the moment.

My fear melts away too, turning into awe as I chance a glance between his shoulder and my cheek.

My eyes widen, my hair whipping around my face, my ponytail holder hanging on for dear life.

This place is beautiful.

Untouched.

Green pine forests stretch across the land below, broken up by rocky, mountainous terrain complete with steep cliffs and more than one river foaming between sharp-edged banks.

I blink, trying to keep my eyes from drying out as the wind buffets us. I'll need some of those goggles aviators used to wear if we're going to be flying often. A stylish choice to be sure. Eat your heart out, Poppy.

A shiver wracks my body, the temperature dropping more the longer he flies. My teeth begin to chatter, and I bite down hard to keep them from clacking.

Still slightly nauseated—whether from the reality of flying bareback with an alien or the devastatingly large number of margaritas last night, I couldn't say—I cling tight to the green alien's body, trying to reposition myself slightly.

Only to encounter what feels like miles of rock-hard muscles.

Whew.

Suddenly, the cold high-altitude air and my lack of proper clothing stop bothering me.

Liquid fire sears through my veins, turning my skin hot and flushed as if I have a fever. The nausea fades too, replaced by something else.

Desire.

And not like, oh shit, I'm crushing on the massive alien I've wrapped myself around.

Nope.

More like, if I don't touch myself right now, immediately, I might spontaneously combust. And if the alien touches me there, I might also spontaneously combust.

I'll put the come in combust.

The mere thought of him touching me is enough to make a fresh wave of fire burn through me.

His nose nuzzles my forehead, and I turn my face back towards him, my eyes widening in embarrassment as moisture seeps through the thin, silky pajama shorts I'm wearing.

What.

The.

Fuck.

I bite my lip, staring into his golden eyes, unable to do more than hang on for dear life as he flies us to lord only knows where, confusingly aroused, sweat beading at the back of my neck.

I need to think about something else.

Anything else.

Work.

Work will do. Excel spreadsheets. Pivot tables.

Oh god, his breath feels good against my forehead. Is that a fang?

I squeeze my eyes shut, worried that if I look into his gorgeous eyes again, I'm going to embarrass myself by coming from that alone.

What the hell is going on with me?

Shit. I'll never look at pivot tables the same way.

Okay, focus, Ellison! This is not the time to get horny. Absolutely not. Sure, he's jacked, but he's an alien, and what's more, you are being flipping filmed.

Embarrassment takes the place of some of my cuckoobird bananapants lust, and I latch onto that for dear life.

How much second-hand embarrassment did I feel when those two *World's Most Eligible* contestants hooked up on camera and the damn producers provided subtitles of their moaning?

I do not want that.

Nope, I do not want any of my moans to be subtitled.

Besides, I don't just hook up with people.

Or aliens.

Subtitles. Dubbed moaning.

Me, writhing in his arms, using his alien dick to get myself off over our pants.

No! Bad brain.

I inhale, my lady parts absolutely aching.

Excel formulas. Having to tell people to turn their mics on during video calls. Telling people to turn their mics off. The Microsoft paperclip help icon.

I squirm, trying to lessen the sensation… and only succeed in moaning again as his fang scrapes against my temple.

Shit. What the hell is going on with my body?

Think, Ellison, think.

Sweat stings my eyes as my alien ride shifts in the air, and a glance down tells me we're descending.

I swallow, tracking the way the ground simply seems to rise up to meet us, too fast. I whimper, and this time, it has nothing to do with the blazing mystery lust trying to make me bone the jolly green giant alien and everything to do with the fact we're coming in too fast.

We have to be coming in too fast.

Our angle changes as the alien starts to dive, and I screech, self preservation taking the reins and my arms scrabbling at him, attempting to climb to his back.

A tiny rational voice in my head tells me this is a bad idea, that trying to ride him like a rodeo clown won't help, seeing as how his freaking wings are on the same damned back I've suddenly attempted to scale—

His tail clamps around my hips, the tip of it between my legs, making my mind go blank with need as it stops just short of where I want it. He rumbles something sharp, the vibration of his voice starting in the lowest part of his chest.

The part my legs are currently spread over.

Sweat beads on my forehead, and my body decides it doesn't give a flying alien fuck about anything but getting off.

I grind against him, whipping my hips up and digging my heels into his back, trying to get him to dip that tail just a liiiiittle bit lower.

Darkness falls, and I squeak in surprise as we accelerate.

Not darkness, no—his wings, the tips of which are now digging into my butt.

My eyes cross as we tumble into the ground, and the force of it is enough to make me climax as he rolls with me tucked up against his chest.

The ability to hold onto him leaves me, and I splat against the ground, my chest heaving, body completely limp.

The alien tilts his head, frowning at me as he stands up.

His tail is still around my waist, and my hips rock up

once more before something zooms across my field of vision and I come back to what's left of my senses.

A drone camera.

We're on reality TV. *Intergalactic* reality TV.

The fact is I just orgasmed against his chest when we hit the ground.

Not to mention the fact that the middle of my pajama shorts now has a damp, darker blue stain spreading across it, and I'm lying spreadeagle on an alien moon.

In the dirt.

"What the hell just happened?" I ask. My gaze tracks over his face until I land on his eyes… which are staring straight at my crotch.

My damp crotch.

Because I just came from falling out of the sky with him.

His nostrils flare, and I clench my teeth together to keep from whimpering. He stands over me, huge, his muscles twitching, his tail locked around me. In the next breath, he's lifting me to my feet.

My legs wobble, and my brain seems to be likewise short-circuiting.

"What is happening to me?" I ask him, practically pawing at his chest in a bid to stay upright.

His tail clamps around me tighter, and I go stock still as he drags his nose down my neck, his breath whuffing across my skin. Claw-tipped fingers tug at my shirt as he works his way across my shoulder.

A shiver goes through me, fresh need coursing across

my skin as if the act of him breathing on me is scrambling my brains.

I back up from him on unsteady feet.

"What the actual hell is going on?" I ask.

I literally came in my pajama pants after falling with him, and now I want more?

Nuh-uh. Not even on my horniest of cycle days is that possible. My poor mental math tells me that I'm not close to that part of my cycle, either.

So something is definitely up, and not just the rock-hard alien boner in his pants.

My eyes narrow to slits, and I cross my arms over my chest, grateful for even the mildest support of my comfiest sleep sports bra.

He steps closer, and I hold up a hand, trying to stop him.

"Do not take another step unless you can tell me why I feel like I'm going to crawl out of my skin if I don't diddle myself right here on the dirt."

I try not to cringe at my poor choice of words.

The winged alien just smiles at me, then says something in his low, growly voice that should not do to me what it does.

I blink, the significance of what I'm hearing finally registering.

"I can't understand you." I shake my head, then poke at my ear. Surely they gave us a translator when they were doing the whole medical check shebang on the flight here. Must be mine's not working.

He says something else, all syllables and consonants that don't mean a single damn thing to me.

Oh, oh no. I was down with the idea of finally getting to try my hand at a set of reality-TV-style challenges. I was even semi-okay with the idea of being paired with an alien instead of one of my friends.

"We can't communicate?" I squawk.

A frown turns his lips down as I continue to put space between us, holding both hands out now.

"We're supposed to do some alien version of all the most ridiculously over-the-top survival shows and we can't even communicate?" It's a screech, and a flock of rainbow-colored birds takes flight in protest.

Shit, shit, triple shit.

I pinch the bridge of my nose, keeping one hand extended as I attempt to calm myself down with deep, cleansing breaths. Isn't that what you're supposed to do to calm down? Breathe?

A delicious, spicy, earthy scent fills my nostrils, and a low moan slips out of me as desire surges. Then a warm, hard stomach presses against my outstretched palm, and I startle.

The smell is coming from him.

The huge, green, winged alien, with a toothy, cocky grin. And a tail. Did I mention the wings?

I cannot believe I signed up for this shit.

Worse, I cannot believe how much I want to knock the green dude in front of me to the ground and have my way with him.

I grind my molars together, a terrible habit that's sure only to give me a fresh headache.

Solving problems? Nope.

Giving myself a headache? Yep.

There's got to be a way out of this, because I'll be damned if I'm gonna rub all over myself or him while being filmed. I don't care how horny I am, that ain't on the freaking to-do list, even if Clippy himself shows up and tries to tell me to get down and dirty.

"No way, no how, paperclip demon!" My back hits something hard, and I sputter as pine needles drop onto my face.

"De-mon?" the alien repeats.

Breathe, breathe, don't scream.

It's not a great mantra, but it's better than giving in to the fire in my blood that seems to demand I jump this strange alien's bones.

Exhibitionism, thou art my nemesis.

If I make it through this, I'm going to cross stich that and hang it on my wall.

The alien's stopped advancing, and he scratches the base of one horn, a confused look on his face. Something drips from the talons on the tips of his wings, steadily hitting the ground under him. Guilt swims through me, and I scrub a hand down my own face. He can't help that I don't speak his language, and he certainly isn't to blame for my body's reaction to him—

Wait.

Wait.

My eyes narrow on the liquid dripping from his

wings. Slowly, my desire-addled brain attempts to put two and two together.

I palm the back of my thighs, which I distinctly remember hurting as we fell from the ship. They don't hurt anymore, but my fingertips are definitely reporting some sort of scratch back there.

"Did you fucking poison me?" I whisper, furious and yet still too damned horny to do more than glare at him.

He takes another step forward, and I karate chop the air between us, baring my teeth. Compared to his, they're really not very intimidating at all, but he should know I mean business. "I invoke the wrath of Clippy," I tell him.

The alien backs up, murmuring things in a calm voice like I'm some kind of rabid animal.

Hell, maybe I am. Who knows what kind of venom this species has? Could be I have alien rabies!

"Clippy?" he repeats, sounding for all the world like he's chewing the name. He points at me. "Clippy?" he repeats, a small, guileless smile replacing his frown.

I blow out a breath, annoyed, because he is *cute* cute, and whether that's the maybe-rabies venom straight-up frying my braincells or a real observation, I don't know.

"No." I shake my head. "No."

"No," he agrees, nodding. He points at me, tilting his head the other way. "No?" he asks, pointing at me again.

I grumble in annoyance. We are *so* not doing the name game right now.

His grin deepens, though, and I squeeze my thighs together, like that's going to solve my problems. News flash: it does not solve anything.

He taps his chest again. "Ka-Rexsh."

Shit. I guess we are doing the name game. I close my eyes, doing my best to repeat my new mantra and get oxygen to my also new wanna-bang-an-alien brain.

"Kaw-wrekch," I try, pointing at him.

He repeats his name, and I do my best to mimic him. Rinse and repeat.

"Kah-rexsh?" I attempt for the tenth time, exasperated.

Finally, he lets out a little laugh, shaking his own head and then nodding and pointing at me. Okay, close enough, then.

"Ellison."

He frowns. "Elleyyzzon."

"My friends call me Ell," I tell him, then scrunch my nose because while we might be paired up, we aren't friends. I might have gotten off against his washboard alien abs, but that doesn't mean we're friends.

Confusion twists his mouth. Not his brow, though, because that forehead is all horn and it ain't moving.

"Ell," I repeat, trying not to get any more frustrated than I already am.

I just have to get through this, and then I'll have scratched off my bucket list item of being on a reality TV show. I need to take it one minute at a time. I blow out a long breath.

"Ell," he repeats. His face lights up as I give him a tentative nod, and I find myself grinning back before I can think better of it.

I wipe the expression off my face as fast as I can,

though, because the big green dude takes another step towards me. I do not need to encourage him to get closer, so I do another karate chop, causing him to stop in his tracks.

I want to ask him about the scratches on my legs, about the stuff that's dripping from the tips of his wings, but I rationally can admit that sort of communication is going to be impossible at this point.

My chest heaves as I sigh.

Alright. Now that we've established what we're going to call each other during this cursed season of *Intergalactic Least Amazing Race*, I take a look around, absorbing our surroundings.

There's a chill in the air, a sort of outdoor icy crisp to it that reminds me of the end of fall. Pine trees stretch as far as I can see, the weak light from whatever sun is in this solar system filtering through various shades of green. A shiver goes through me, and I fervently wish I'd worn something warmer to sleep in. I'm no Girl Scout, seeing as how things like that pretty much dried up after the Roth invasion, but I know one thing for certain in my bones.

It's going to be frigid once the sun goes down tonight.

And all I have on are these thin Hawaiian floral print pajamas to keep warm.

That, and the near-blinding heat scorching me from the inside out, turning my lady parts achy all over again the minute I think about it.

Holding my hands up, in an attempt to keep him from touching me, I take a few steps towards him, and then reach up on my tip toes to point at the tip of the webbed wing closest to me.

His eyes narrow as he tracks my movement.

I jab my finger at the talon again, then swivel so he can see the backs of my legs and point at the scratches there.

He scratches at the base of his horn again.

I repeat the motion, pointing at the tip of his dripping talon, and then to my scratches, waiting for him to tell me something I know I won't be able to understand anyway.

This is getting old really fast.

I start to do it again, pointing to his talons and to my legs—mind getting duller by the moment, heat getting, well, hotter, by the moment, too—when his arms scoop me up, and those dripping talons scrape down my back.

My eyes roll back in my head at the pure fucking pleasure of it, another orgasm building from the pressure of his talons on my skin alone.

Heat builds, his mere touch fanning the flames I'd done a pretty okay job of keeping at bay, when it clicks.

If there was any doubt that whatever is dripping from his wings was making me horny, it's gone now. I'm about five seconds away from sticking my hands down my shorts and finishing myself off.

My breathing's rapid, and his golden eyes devour me as I stare up at him, open-mouthed, needing him frantically, knowing in my head that it's not real, that it's some biological response to what he's done, when a strange beeping song fills the air around us.

A drone plunges into the clearing, and Ka-Rexsh

growls, pulling me into his side and wrapping a wing around me protectively.

My heart skips a beat because I might not ever admit it again, but being treated like a fragile little princess might just do it for me. It's either that or the maybe-rabies venom melting my neural pathways.

Who's to say?

I am a connoisseur of all things alien fanfic, and though this would tick a few of my favorite tag boxes in a story, living it is an entirely different kettle of fish.

I peek out from around his wing, trying my very best not to hump his tree-trunk thigh and mostly succeeding, and catch sight of a thick chunk of writing. In bold letters, a logo screams across the drone's shell in English, and then again in the same font in a language I can't make heads or tails of.

I force my hips still mid-hump, my jaw going slack, the headache redoubling behind my eyes.

Mated and Afraid.

"Oh, *shit*."

It dawns on me at the same time the alien nuzzles the top of my head with his nose, murmuring alien nonsense at my obvious distress.

"Fuck me sideways and call me Clippy."

We're not just partners. We're not mates in the way Australians mean it, either.

Nope.

We're *mated*-mated, in the way a lot of the alien species mean it. I've done minimal actual research on the few alien species we know about on Earth, thanks to the

Federation declassifying some of their documents a couple years ago. Binging fanfic about aliens only gets you so far in the old knowledge bin, but thanks to that, mated is absolutely a term I'm familiar with.

It's the most common alien fanfic trope, after all.

Mated means forever to most of them.

Which means that it isn't maybe-rabies venom.

I swallow hard, staring at the metal box emblazoned with that colorful logo.

It was mating venom, and if my alien fanfic habit has taught me anything all, it's that the venom's started something pretty damned serious.

I'm in deep shit, and—I'm in heat.

CHAPTER SIX

KA-REXSH

Everything is going very nicely, I think.

My female is tucked under my wing after asking for a second dose of my mating venom. The scent of her heat is driving me out of my mind with lust, the sweet, spicy scent of her cunt calling to me.

I am being very patient, though.

I will not mate with her until she asks me to.

From the way she's currently rubbing her damp heat against my thigh, though, I think perhaps she will ask me to soon.

My cock jumps at the idea, beginning to skith again.

The drone that's frightened my human mate buzzes in front of us, and I hold out a hand. A second later, the metal box drops into my palm, and I open the lid with a flick of my claw.

My little mate is making words in her strange language, and I mentally curse the Roth organizers of this game for not allowing us translator technology.

A few moments go by and I frown, staring into the empty box—then nearly drop it as a voice booms out of it, an image projecting in the interior, some sort of hologram.

"Welcome to *Mated and Afraid*," the hologram in the box says, a wide grin on his face. I squint at the image.

It's odd, the hologram—it looks human sometimes, Roth or even Suevan next, the image flickering between forms as I watch.

We watch, I correct myself, because the beautiful female at my side is gazing up at the image open-mouthed. I tear my gaze away from those petal-pink lips and force myself to listen to the machine.

"The concept is simple, but the contest will not be." The hologram smiles even wider, and something about it makes me want to growl. "Five challenges, all along different routes on this Suevan-system moon. Travel by air is not allowed, so you'll be taking your mate through the wilderness while you adapt to the environment… and to each other."

I sneak another glance at the perfect female by my side, and she's looking between the hologram and me with an angry, wrinkled forehead.

Seeing the lines and furious pout on her mouth makes me want to laugh and smooth her forehead out all at once.

I do not know if she'd like that, though, so I focus on

the hologram and settle for rubbing the hard bone plate under the horns on my own forehead.

"Each challenge will have a reward, but the first is probably the most important—a translator for you and your mate, as well as two packs of supplies that will greatly ease the rest of your journey." The hologram pauses dramatically, making a great show of looking down at a large apparatus strapped to its wrist. "The first challenge begins at nightfall. You have three hours to make it to the first waypoint. If you aren't there before nightfall, you will forfeit the challenge—and the chance to have a translator by the end of the day." The hologram fizzles out.

A translation device, within our grasp.

Happiness makes my wings curl up tight, and I smile down at my little human female just as the voice starts again, this time in the strange tones of her language.

She slides her gaze from my face to the box in my hand, watching the hologram with a rapt expression. I find myself lost in the minutiae of her face.

It's so expressive compared to the Draegon I've spent my life around. I can practically see the thoughts flit across her face, her eyebrows and forehead moving with every new piece of information the hologram reveals.

Finally, she slumps against me as the hologram finishes the speech in her strange language. The humans brought to my planet centuries ago speak Draegon, as does everyone there, so the communicator they've promised as a prize for our first challenge will be useful indeed.

Something is wrong with this place.

I cannot quite puzzle out what is so off—there's no wildlife, no noise at all, but it's more than that.

This place is just wrong.

A drone buzzes around us, interrupting my thoughts, and I fight the urge to snarl at it and bring it down. It would be so easy; a pump of my wings, a swipe of my talons, and the threat would be dealt with. I do not want anyone seeing my perfect mate but me.

Already, the urge to rut her has begun, made worse by the delicious, spiced scent of her heat. It grows stronger by the second, tantalizing and mouthwatering and teasing me beyond all hope of rational thought.

I must be calm.

I take a deep breath, but it only makes it worse, her delectable scent bombarding my senses.

Every attempt I've made to calm myself has not worked, though, and the only thing somewhat settling me is the feel of my female against my skin.

A female with whom I am unable to communicate, but whose body feels as perfect as can be pressed up against mine.

CHAPTER SEVEN

ELLISON

I fan my face, trying not to think about how good the alien behind me feels. The thick muscles of his stomach provide the perfect place to lean against, and one wayward hand wraps casually around his thigh as if we've known each other for our whole lives.

Gritting my teeth, I force my hand away. There is no reason on Earth, er, on this random-ass moon, that I should be rubbing myself all over him like a cat in heat.

Except for the fact that I am a *human* in heat.

I scrub a palm down my face, feeling feverish, a light sheen of sweat coating my skin. It's uncomfortable, a prickling sensation that reminds me vaguely of the time I ran into a patch of poison ivy as a kid and didn't realize what I'd done until it was much, much too late.

"It's going to get worse, isn't it?" The question comes

out on a moan, and I lurch away from him, the movement as sloppy as if I were still nose-deep in a pitcher of frozen margaritas.

I wince at the mere thought of more tequila, my stomach flip-flopping.

Ew. I put a hand over my mouth, like that's going to stop my intestinal revolt.

Big ew.

Ka-Rexsh tilts his head, the small stretch of skin between his eyebrows furrowing just slightly, as if the horns protruding above them stop him from a full-on scowl.

"Mates?" I ask, weary already of all that single word entails, knowing he can't understand me but needing to talk it out.

Well, can't be any more one-sided than the last conversation I had with an ex-boyfriend! A mirthless cackle erupts from my mouth, which is better than the other substance that threatened to erupt.

I cock my head at the big alien. At least Ka-Rexsh has a reason for not responding: he can't understand me.

Alan, the last guy I dated, could.

He was just a run-of-the-mill human asshole.

I arch an eyebrow, my gaze running over Ka-Rexsh's body. There's nothing run-of-the mill about him, and his gorgeous body is also *definitely* an upgrade. Plus, the heated way Ka-Rexsh is looking at me makes my skin tingle all over.

Alan definitely never looked at me like that—like he wanted to eat me up.

Not that I'm truly considering being his mate. I'm not. Nope.

My gaze drops lower, to the definite bulge in his pants, and when I bite my lip, he hisses out a breath. I glance back up at him, his pupils dilating as I watch.

"I didn't sign up for this," I tell him, my voice wobbling. "I didn't know I was getting a mate, or going into heat, or fuck—" I rake my hand through my hair, which is impossibly snarled from flying here.

Flying.

In a dragon alien's arms.

My dragon alien *mate*.

Ka-Rexsh.

I swallow hard, dizzy and hot—the flush of what can only be the induced heat making me feverish, and strange—like my skin fits just slightly too tight.

"Hot," I manage, my voice thick and husky and unusual to my own ears. I fan my face, and when he stalks closer to me, I freeze.

I so do not want to jump his bones.

I mean, I so *do* want to jump his bones, but that would mean sealing the mate bond that's already starting to form, and I don't even know him.

He can't want this either.

I don't know much about the alien species besides the Suevans and the Roth, and the Draegon—or Drazox—are arguably some of the most secretive.

Maybe he was abducted too. Maybe he was forced to be here, and he doesn't want me at all.

The thought chills some of the lava-temperature desire coursing through my veins.

I blow out a giant breath, trying to hold onto that thought, onto some semblance of sanity. Yeah, that's it. Someone coerced him to be here, and he's disgusted by me.

My nose crinkles at the idea of it.

Success!

Mind over matter, that's all this is.

I toss a hand into the air, palm out, in what I hope is the literal universal signal for stop. Stop, because if he takes another step closer to me, I might just get down on my knees and beg him to fuck me.

Urgh.

That was the wrong mental image. I squeeze my eyes shut, like that will help block my stupid, stubborn brain.

Crossing one leg over the other, I try to Kegel my lust into oblivion. It turns out, however, that that's not a thing, not at all.

At least my lady tunnel will be toned if I ever decide to open her up for business.

I manage to open one eye, and his lips are turned down into a frown, his pointy canines no longer apparent.

Good. I'm much less likely to think about how hot he is if he looks more like a human douche-knuckle.

My nose scrunches up. I don't know what that word means.

"Dooosh nuckelle?" Ka-Rexsh asks in a plaintive tone.

My jaw drops, and then I snap my mouth shut. Amazing.

I said it out loud, and he's repeating the shitty made-up word like some wayward alien toddler.

The urge to scream makes me clamp my molars together with a loud clack.

His eyebrows nudge up, both horns raising slightly with them.

"I'm not into this," I hiss at him, keeping my hand palm out and shaking my head. "I didn't ask to be put into some alien heat. I didn't ask for a mate. For a lifetime!"

I scowl, pausing, because I did, in fact, sign up for this.

I just skipped the fine print.

"Shit," I say, attempting to run my hand through my hair again and failing. I tug my hand out, and manage to pull a ton of loose hair out at the same time. Ew. I shake out my hand, letting the strands fall to the soft earthen ground.

Today is not my day.

A ragged sigh rips out of me.

At least whatever the Roth shot me up with when they told us where we were and showed us the paperwork we'd signed has burned off what was sure to be an unholy hangover.

"Shit," Ka-Rexsh repeats unhelpfully.

"Shit." I nod emphatically. "Good pronunciation on that one."

He beams at me, and damn if my legs don't try to turn to jelly at the way the smile transforms his face.

"Alright," I say, making up my mind. My hands fly to my hips, and my mouth scrunches to the side. Overhead, the drone buzzes loudly as it zooms closer. "If I'm here, I'm going to do this. Did I want a mate? No!" I yell, slashing an X with my hands in front of my body. He blinks.

Too loud, okay.

He nods encouragingly, though, and I clear my throat before beginning again.

"No, I did not," I repeat, because I need to remember that no matter what Little Miss Pussy Galore down below is telling my brain, we are not banging. We are so not banging the hot dragon alien. "Did I know that we would be abducted and put on an alien planet for this show immediately? No!"

"No," he agrees, just repeating the word like a hot dragon parrot.

I snap my fingers at him. "Exactly. But now that I'm here, am I going to let that stop me from winning?"

"No," he yells at me, and I nod fervently, pacing and talking with my hands, like I can mime my way into communicating with him.

"So we can't fly," I flap my arms at him, and his eyes widen. "And we aren't going to bang," I say, doing some very illustrative hip-thrusting. "But we can fucking win!" I yell, throwing my arms into a victory V. "And if there's one absolutely terrible thing about me, it's how competitive I am. I will ruin friendships over Monopoly." I mime throwing dice, still pacing. My tone is increasingly unhinged, but I'm going with it. "And don't even get me started on Scrabble. If you can't spell well, you best not take on the queen."

I place an imaginary crown on my head, then pretend to sit my ass on a throne. Nearly immediately, my thighs start to shake, so I abandon the fake throne pretty damn quick.

He stares at me.

I stare at him.

He blinks, then descends upon me in a flurry of whirling limbs and wings.

"What the fuck?" I squeak, taking a step back and falling straight on my ass.

CHAPTER EIGHT

KA-REXSH

My little human mate is attempting a mating dance.

It is clumsy, and it is not the way of my people, but she is enthusiastic and loud. I am thoroughly charmed by her alien efforts.

I knew the people of her planet were primitive, yes, so far behind in the sciences and evolution that they have nearly no skills to speak of, but I did not know that they still used something as strange as a mating dance.

Still.

What else could it possibly be? She is adorable, with her nonsense burbling and her cute hornless head as she squats and touches her temple.

She pauses, her expressive eyebrows quirking up, her brown eyes wide as her appreciative gaze skates over my skin.

I brush off the feeling of awkwardness, and snap my wings to their fullest extension, doing my best to perform a dance that is sure to impress the strange little human.

Spinning on my heels, I advance towards her, trying not to grimace at my clumsy interpretation of what I'm sure is a time-honored mating ritual of her species. What I lack in choreography and precision I try to make up for with sheer enthusiasm.

I close my eyes, losing my inhibitions to movement, and by the time I finish and open my eyes, I know I've done my very best. My heart skips within my chest, so eager for her reaction to my overtures in a way she will understand.

My mate stares up at me from the ground, her lush lips round with surprise.

"Whaattheefaack?" she screeches, scrabbling back like a rock crab on her palms and feet.

My eyes narrow.

She watches me carefully, a skittish expression on her face. That is not the reaction I anticipated.

Perhaps the human mating dance is more complicated than I thought. Perhaps they have many dances and I've just offered her a grave insult.

I scratch my chin, confused about where I went wrong.

I have never been a male to give up in the face of hardship. I wouldn't be here if I were.

Recalling her movements, I slow down, attempting to repeat what she did. Her face twists up as I squat, touching my horns, then stand back up.

A moment passes.

Another.

We stare at one another.

Finally I huff in annoyance at myself.

She must not have been doing a mating dance, after all. I am a brainless worm for having made such an assumption. Behind me, my wings sag, and I bow my head, my heart falling, even the relentless skith of my cock ceasing as reality sets in.

Ellison might be in heat for me, might have agreed to do this contest, but if she were truly interested in being my mate, she would have responded to me in the way of a mate by now.

My palm scrubs across my face because I have never wanted something so badly as I want the female before me, the scent of her heat starting a reaction in my own veins—but I refuse to take.

I have had too much taken from me in my life to do the same to another.

Especially the one I have marked as my own.

My hand stretches out to her, practically of its own accord, and her eyes narrow. Darting between my sharp-taloned fingers and my face, her gaze flicks back and forth until she finally stands on her own.

As if she doesn't trust the merest touch.

"Come," I tell her, letting my hand fall to my side. "We must make haste to the first stage of the competition."

It's strange, not being able to fly where I want, but if we want to win, we must abide by the rules set forth by the Roth.

I want to win. I want to win the translator so I can know what is happening in her pretty head.

But I want to win more than this competition—I want to win my mate over, body and soul.

I started this journey for the chance to get away from the autocratic Draegon politics, but this female? She is the true prize I seek.

CHAPTER NINE

ELLISON

My legs are shaking.

Straight up trembling. Sweat slicks every inch of my skin, dirt clinging to me more easily with every fresh drop.

The terrain is harsh, and the soles of my bare feet are peppered with cuts and bruises already. Overhead, blue sky peeks out above tall trees, a distant planet hanging large in the sky, visible even now.

It's darker, though, darker every time I glance up.

And I'm glancing up a lot, because I'll be damned if I look at Ka-Rexsh's delicious wide shoulders and biceps up ahead of me.

His wings are pulled in tight, huge enough that they cover the perfect bubble of his ass.

I lick my lips, then glance back up at the darkening sky.

Feverish. That's how I feel. Light-headed, bizarre, out-of-sorts. Hot, then cold, goosebumps chasing sweat, my feet painful.

My teeth grind together, and I purse my lips into a thin line.

I refuse to complain.

I am not a whiner. I always get annoyed when a contestant on one of the shows I watch won't shut up about how bad they have it, as if they didn't sign up to be there. As if they didn't know what they were in for when they signed up to be stranded on the side of a volcano.

I'll be damned if I get labeled the whiner on this season, even though I did not know what I was getting myself into.

Just one more minute, I tell my aching feet.

I have no idea if it's a minute or not, but everything seems more bearable in terms of taking it one minute at a time.

I tilt my head, cracking my neck. Eyes closed, I inhale deeply, regretting all those mornings I lay in bed snoozing the alarm on my phone instead of hitting the gym.

Although no amount of working out normally could have prepared me for shoeless adventures in heat on an alien planet.

I swallow a sigh, trudging onward. One more minute. I can do one more minute.

And then one more minute.

And then

Cold droplets splatter on my cheeks, and my foot stops mid-stride as I crane my neck, looking up. Grey clouds push out the blue sky, still deepening as the day wears into night.

More rain falls, and I shiver as it splatters across my skin.

"If it stays sprinkling like this, it won't be so bad," I tell myself over the lump in my throat.

Ka-Rexsh turns around, taking in my upturned face with a curious expression. Or, at least, what I interpret as curious. Who the hell knows what that expression means on an alien?

Not me, that's for damn sure.

He utters something in his language, and I cock my head, like that will suddenly make the words make sense. Newsflash: it does not.

"We should hurry," I tell him. What felt good at first, the icy rain slowly spattering across my skin, has quickly turned extremely uncomfortable.

My teeth begin to chatter.

He takes a few steps toward me, and I clamp my mouth shut—which just causes the rest of my body to pick up the shaking.

"Drezzex shen K'lata zet?" he says, the little bit of his brow that can furrow doing so as he stares at me. His strange gold-orange eyes seem to swirl the longer I stare into them. So pretty.

The palm of my hand heats, and I blink as I realize I've reached up to touch his face.

"Shagrette leszzmeist," he says on a growl, biting off the words.

Words that make absolutely no sense whatsoever to me.

Huge hands bracket my waist, and then he's lifting my shivering body, holding me close.

The sky goes completely dark—at least, that's what I think in a moment of sheer panic—but it's his wings. He's holding them over me like a heated umbrella, and as the rain begins to fall in earnest, heavier and heavier, I decide that being curled up in the alien's warm and dry arms is much preferable to having to haul ass on my bare feet to the first challenge.

I sigh, pressing my cheek against his deliciously hot skin, the chattering of my teeth coming and going randomly as he lopes along, much faster now that I'm not trailing behind him at a snail's pace.

Part of me feels slightly guilty about him carrying me, but the longer he's at it, the clearer it becomes that I was slowing him down to an ungodly pace. His breathing is even and easy, and he vaults through the rocky forest terrain with so much ease that watching him is… delightful.

All those muscles.

That tail, whipping back and forth to balance him. The wings, arched over our heads to keep me dry.

No complaints from me, none at all.

He's muttering to me, a steady stream of guttural nonsense words that I can make neither head nor tails of, and between the sound of the pelting rain on his wings, the motion of his run, and the fact that I feel warm, warm and... safe, my eyes get heavier with each second that slides by.

Safe.

I'm on an alien planet, filming an adventure reality show, mating heat coursing through my veins—and I feel safer with this giant winged male than any boyfriend I've ever tried to sleep next to in my life.

I don't know if the heat has something to do with it, or if it's real, but I snuggle closer and for once in my life, I decide I don't care. I don't care, and I'm going to take advantage of it, and rest while I can.

I have no idea how much I'm going to need it, either.

CHAPTER
TEN

KA-REXSH

Ellison snores lightly, like a small, furry mammal some of the richer Draegon keep as pets. Her pretty pink lips fall open in sleep, her face relaxed and so arrestingly beautiful that I nearly trip over a felled tree as I stare down at her in a heady mix of lust and pure wonder.

My mate.

Asleep, in my arms, as though there is nothing that can harm her while I hold her tight.

Her trust is precious to me.

Her body is soft and small, and the scent of the heat on her is driving me half wild, pushing me to touch her.

Joy rises in me anew, at the possibility of our pairing, of our future together.

It solidifies my resolve. I will win this contest for her, for us.

It is a way off my planet, out of my life of servitude to the mad king, and in my arms is the key to everything I want.

A female of my own, a future with her, a future where I can live for myself, for us both.

It's all I have ever wanted, and the first piece is sleeping in my arms, her heat calling to every fiber of my being.

My feet move faster still, as if the quicker a pace I set, the sooner we get to the first challenge, the sooner I can claim my mate and my future.

I want to tell her all I have planned.

I want to hear her words, understand how to dance for her in the way of her people, so that she will come into my arms willingly again, so I can taste the delectable scent rising from her skin already.

I am not sure there is any pace fast enough to soothe the need inside me.

CHAPTER
ELEVEN

ELLISON

Groggy, I sit up—or try to. Ka-Rexsh places a huge hand over my mouth as I struggle against him, trying to get my bearings.

I go still immediately, my eyes wide as my memories of the day rush back to me.

Reality TV.

Mated and Afraid.

The first challenge.

I'm in heat.

As if summoned by my thoughts, my entire body shivers with the need for relief, and not any that Tylenol could provide.

Not unless that's what my big ole alien dragon is shooting out his—

I clear my throat, tearing my gaze away from where my hip's pressed against his lower abdomen.

It would be so easy to just pull the leg of my pajama pants wide, tug his pants down, and shove him right up in there. My lower body tightens at the mere idea, and I lick my lips.

My lips, which are still covered by his hand.

I just licked his hand.

I grimace, and he stares down at me with those wild orange and gold eyes, a soft exhalation on his lips.

"Challenge?" I whisper, forgetting he can't understand me.

Yeah, that seriously blows. We need to win whatever this is so we can communicate.

I shift slightly in his arms, quiet as I can be, my spine tingling with the sense that silence is very, very important right now. Slowly, so slowly, I turn my head, fear making my heart slam against my ribs.

My fingers curl into his shoulders.

What is it that has him afraid, this huge, muscled alien?

Maybe we have to fight some sort of awful alien monster, or a lion, or go through an obstacle course over lava—

I blink, narrowing my eyes at the sight that has my mate, er, dragon alien partner, silent and crouching in the underbrush.

Lights cascade over a shining platform, an audience of Roth and green-scaled Suevans alike chatting amicably in front of it.

What the hell are the Roth and Suevans doing here? And chatting... with each other?

I swallow hard. Sure, the Federation told us all that the Suevans and Roth had brokered a peace treaty, that the leader who ravaged our planet had been replaced with someone less homicidal, but it's one thing to hear it from the international government who basically threw women at the Suevans for technology, and another to see it with my own eyes.

My gaze drifts from the assembled all-male crowd back up to the smooth-surfaced platform, where a bevy of lights shimmer across the surface.

The truth of it hits me like a ton of bricks.

It's a stage.

A stage?!

"What the fuck?" I breathe, only to have a huge hand clap over my mouth. Ka-Rexsh drags me up against his body, and I squirm, trying to get free.

Mostly because nobody puts baby in a corner—er, a hand over my mouth—but also because being pressed flush against his chest with his hands all over me is doing very delicious things to my body.

Delicious but also things that I do not need to be doing while filmed.

Cheese and crackers.

Ka-Rexsh is too late, though, because even my miniscule exhalation of a curse has attracted attention.

The nearest Suevan and Roth, sitting in the back corner, both stand at once, their handsome alien faces much more normal to me than the Draegon I'm currently cowering against. My body positively ignites at the idea of three handsome-as-hell dudes all staring me down, and I let loose a whimper.

A whimper that causes something very hard and long to rock against my ass.

I go still, my eyes wide.

Because whatever that is on my dragon dude... it's moving. Squirming even, like a huge boa constrictor I was forced to hold at a fifth-grade field trip to the local zoo.

I do not like that, no sirree, I do not like that at all.

Some memories are best left repressed.

I squeal, pushing away from him with strength I didn't know I had, tumbling straight into the arms of the Suevan standing in front of me. His eyes go wide, and I recoil slightly as I stare up at him, a third eyelid winking over his pupil, his alligator-like tail whipping behind him.

The Roth says something under his breath, and the Suevan snarls at him in response.

I cringe away because even though my body is begging to be touched, their touch doesn't feel right, not at all.

A rough voice grates across my ears, and taloned fingers prick through the flimsy fabric of my dirty pajama top as Ka-Rexsh pulls me back against him.

If I moan a little, frickin' sue me. I'm in heat, and everything about my big Draegon alien protector partner just feels right.

Honestly, I'd be enjoying it if it weren't for two pretty glaring problems: one, the fact that the two of us are making a scene, and two, the fact that I'm becoming increasingly sure that the boa constrictor in his pants is not a boa constrictor at all.

"Is that a snake in your pants or are you just happy to see me?" I choke out, then let out a high-pitched, manic excuse for a laugh that leaves the Roth and Suevan cringing at the noise.

Ka-Rexsh just holds me tighter, though, still snarling what sounds like threats to the other two aliens.

A remote, detached part of me can't help but think this is going to make for great reality TV. Heck, maybe it will make it into a promo reel.

"Oh, there they are! They beat us here after all," a familiar voice says.

Relief leaves me sagging against Ka-Rexsh as Poppy appears on stage, looking fresh as a daisy and as gorgeous as always. Her plumps cheek are bit pink, and maybe there is a trace of dirt along her thigh, but otherwise, she seems completely at ease and camera-ready.

My hands clench into fists as she glances over the alien holding me upright.

That's my alien, and she shouldn't be looking at him at all.

I shake my head, confusion replacing the possessive thought.

The heat. It's got to be the heat, right? Poppy may have fucked up royally by entering us into this mess, but she's my friend.

Besides, based on the way she looks coquettishly through her lashes at the brawny red alien Draegon holding her hand, she is clearly not interested in mine.

A bit more of the odd possessiveness clears, and I blink, staring at Poppy and the red-winged alien on stage.

Since when did I start thinking of Ka-Rexsh as mine?

CHAPTER
TWELVE

KA-REXSH

My female pats my bicep, then strokes it, the heat of her fingertips finally making me avert my aggressive stare from the Suevan who dared touch her.

Her hand feels heavenly on my skin, and I take a long moment to savor it.

"Rex," she says, and the side of my mouth lifts in a smug smirk as I realize she's given me a nickname.

Only the most affectionate of breeding pairs give each other nicknames, and my cock likes that very, very much So much that it skiths even harder, pulsing against the firm expanse of her back. The bud of pleasure even begins to pucker at the base of my cock, something it's never done for another, and never will.

This human mate is the only one for me.

My Ellison.

The truth of it is like the toll of a bell through me, and I tuck her into my body, my wings flaring around us as I lean down and bury my nose in her hair, inhaling her intoxicating musk.

How is it that I cannot even communicate with my Ellison, but I am already a wing's tip away from obsession with her?

The Roth takes a step towards us, and I jerk her away from him, snarling again, nearly fully feral in my need to keep her away from them.

"Come now, all contestants to the stage, please," the Roth from the ship, from before my Ell chose me, stands on stage, a smile plastered over the lingering smell of his uncertainty.

The Roth instigator should be more than uncertain. My wings tremble with the need to teach him a lesson, to show everyone that she is mine.

A mechanized voice repeats his words in what I assume is the females' language, and Ell pushes against my arms as she attempts to follow his directions.

She's not leaving my side, not when I am beginning to feel the pull of my rut answering her heat.

Hooking an arm around the curve of her waist, I lift her easily, and she makes an adorable squeak of surprise.

I lower my mouth to her ear as I pad towards the stage, knowing all the males assembled here are watching us, waiting for a glimpse of *my* female.

Mine.

The last thing I want is for anyone else's eyes to be on her. She is mine to look at, mine to cherish, mine to touch.

The red Draegon on stage averts his eyes politely, his lightly furred tail flicking behind him. I jerk my chin at him in a sign of respect as I carry my prize forward, avoiding looking at the female beside him. He pulls her closer anyway, the fluffed end of his tail wrapping around her waist. The side of his lip curls in a snarl, and I scent his mate's response to him.

Too sweet for me, much too sugary.

No, I prefer the spice and smokey undertones of my mate to this one.

I lean forward again, her light brown hair tickling my nostrils as I inhale her, dragging my nose against her scalp as she shivers, skin heating.

Gods, but this female sings to my blood, everything about her making my body respond.

The true trial of this contest will not be making it to the end—it will be avoiding my rut until my female wants me as much as I need her.

CHAPTER
THIRTEEN

ELLISON

Being held by good ole Rex is a problem. Hearing him breathe is a problem.

The feel of his breath on my scalp is a problem.

But the biggest problem of all is the massive, pulsating dick pushed up against my back, so stiff it's lifting my pajama shirt along with his pants—and the fact that I'm getting slick between my legs in some heat-induced chemical reaction.

I didn't learn about the Draegon laws of sex thermodynamics in school, but I'm getting a front-row crash course to it now regardless.

Alien Pheromone Sex Thermodynamics 101, 102, and grad school thesis, all in one neat reality show timeline.

I've always been an overachiever.

A hysterical laugh tries to burble out of me, but I

clamp my lips shut. If I let a laugh out at this predicament, who knows what will happen next? Nope. It's time to do my very best corporate robot impression, and put all my practice on those deadly-boring video conferences to good use.

From a small slit between Rex's wings, I can still make out Poppy and her red-hued guy, as well as the Roth from the spaceship.

The announcer, I presume.

Selene isn't here, or her Draegon alien, and I frown, worry for the pair of them rushing through me. Did they not make it in time? Are they okay?

Surely nothing too serious could have happened to delay them; this is reality TV, not an actual survival situation… right? I mean, I can't shake the feeling that this whole planet, er moon, er place is weird, but that's probably because it's just not Earth.

The questions running through my head stop suddenly, my breath hitching as Rex sets me down. My pajama shirt wriggles loose and falls over the top of his hand— qhich means his palm is on my bare skin.

Oh, yum.

Whimpering, I squeeze my upper thighs together. Good grief, why did I have to wear pajama shorts? If I get any wetter, it's going to slide down my legs for the whole universe to see.

Rex tilts his head, and I swallow hard, seeing him assess me from the corner of my eye.

Even from this angle, his lips look ridiculously kissable. My eyes go wide, and I squirm slightly, only to force myself to stifle another moan as his hand presses into the curve of my stomach. Normally, I'd be sucking it in and trying to make sure that whoever was touching me didn't think about how long it had been since I'd done any sort of core workout.

In Rex's arms, though? I simply don't care what he thinks about my soft midsection. Based on the way he feels against me, he doesn't mind at all—nah, the opposite seems to be true.

He likes my squishy, imperfect middle.

A bubble of warmth that has nothing to do with lust goes through my chest. He likes the way I look and feel. Mating heat or not, that's a pretty damned nice feeling.

It sure as heck would be nice to have a man who loves all my imperfections instead of one who constantly sees my body as their own personal fitness coaching challenge.

Emotion tightens my throat, unbidden tears stinging my eyes.

I dash them away with the back of my hand.

"Hormones," I tell myself. It's gotta be the mating heat making me all squishy and soft towards him. That's all this is.

"Oh my god, you two are okay." Lily stumbles onto the stage.

I push Rex's wing aside a little, and though he gives a rumbling growl of displeasure, he allows me more room to look at my friend. A purplish scarred Draegon with silvery-white hair storms after her, leaves and sticks falling out of Lily's hair like she's been tumbling around on the ground. Her knees are skinned too, dried blood crusting her shins.

"What happened to you?" I ask, taken aback.

Her gaze drops, and she rakes her fingers through her short, wavy black hair. Another leaf falls out, and she glares at it.

"I fell," she says.

My eyes narrow. "Uh-huh."

"Thank fuck this is the translator challenge," Lily does her best to ignore the alien dragon staring at her with open desire. "Not being able to talk to this dude is driving me fucking nuts."

"You're on TV," Poppy tells her in a scandalized voice. "Watch your mouth."

"Don't even fucking start with me, Poppy," Lily tells her, pure venom in her tone. The Draegon alien tailing her gives Poppy an unfriendly look, his biceps bulging as he reaches for Lily, who manages to slither from his grasp.

"Hi, you guys," Lucy says, all sunshine and cheer as her Draegon alien bridal-carries her up the stairs. "These guys are handy to have around, huh?"

"More like handsy," Lily mutters, casting a dark look at the male next to her. He bares his fangs at her, tail lashing behind him, and she rolls her eyes. "Knock it off, loser."

Rex chuckles behind me, and I guess he doesn't need a translator to pick up on her disdain and her partner's— no, mate's—annoyance.

It hits me then. I don't feel disdainful of Ka-Rexsh, not at all. Worried and anxious about being in heat, yes. But he's been kind, and helpful, and being able to communicate is definitely what we need if we're going to make it to the end and win.

Not to mention it will help us lay some ground rules about, er, touching.

Heat sizzles through my veins.

I refuuuuse to give in to it, though, even if the evidence of the damned heat is soaking into my pajama shorts after I swipe my sweaty palms against them.

"Welcome to the inaugural season of *Mated and Afraid*," the Roth at the front of the stage booms out, his voice amplified by some technology that I can't see. "And welcome to our first challenge!"

Unease threads through me, and as if he can sense it, Rex leans low, murmuring words I can't understand against my ear.

A shiver of something I don't want to put a name to goes down my spine.

Lily catches my eye, and we share a nervous glance even as Poppy beams into the crowd of assembled aliens.

Maybe Poppy knows what all the challenges are already. A scowl furrows my forehead. I love Poppy, but damn, I'm not real happy with her at the moment.

"We will begin the challenge by letting you each randomly select your event."

My scowl turns into a cringe, because if there's random chance involved in these events, that means some of the choices will, without a doubt, be absolutely horrific. Will we be forced to eat larvae? Swim blindfolded through a cave? Go skydiving naked?

Rex's wing rustles near my face, and I mentally cross out naked skydiving because I don't think the Draegon would find that anything but commonplace.

Probably even the naked part.

Something under the stage squeals, and I jump back in surprise, Rex's arms tightening around me as a gap opens up in the platform.

I squint reflexively as lights flash from the object now being raised onto the platform, and then my jaw drops open.

It's a wheel—one of those multicolored carnival-style wheels, designed to spin on a selection. Each different segment contains two types of writing—English, and what I can only assume is written Draegon scrawled above it.

Resolve tightens my chest.

I really, really want to win this damn thing.

Rex murmurs something unintelligible—because everything is unintelligible when you don't speak the same language—his fingers and talons lightly stroking the skin on my hip. The dual sensation sends goosebumps skittering over my skin.

If this were one of my fanfictions, we would fall madly in love after he saved me from some disaster, and then I would be rewarded for my bravery in kissing an alien with the best orgasm of my life.

Call me delulu, because part of me wants that to be true-true. Or, more accurately, call me in heat, because my libido is out of fucking control.

I shift nervously, trying to ignore the way Rex's

sniffing my hair is making me even more hot and bothered.

This isn't a fanfic, and I didn't sign up to go into heat, and I'm sure as shit not going to get distracted from the grand prize by something as fleeting as an orgasm.

I clear my throat, the noise high and squeaky.

Poppy's gaze flits to me, and there's worry in her big blue eyes. She bites her bottom lip nervously, then grins as the big red Draegon behind her tugs it out of her grasp.

A strange ache rolls across my chest, and I rub at it, then startle as I realize the Roth host is gesturing Rex and me forward.

"Approach and spin the wheel," the mechanized translator announces.

Rex pulls me close to him, practically carrying me over to where the host has indicated. He's still mostly blocking me from the view of the all-male Roth and Suevan audience, and the view of whoever is watching at home.

Huh. I peek out again—why aren't there any Draegon in the audience? Weird.

His wing moves, and my temporary view is obscured. Considering I'm still wearing my jammies and a bit worse for wear after our jaunt here, I'm not even a little bit upset about it. Likewise, considering I'm a complete horndog, I might even relish it.

My nose scrunches up, and I try to distract myself by staring up at the flashing monstrosity of a game show wheel and reading the descriptions in the segments.

That's the ticket; I need something to focus on.

Unfortunately, reading the descriptions only intensifies my apprehension.

"Style build and drag?" I read out loud. "Puzzle organ fun? Lost in ice?" What the actual… "These must be mistranslated," I say, directing the comment at the host.

He just smiles at me, his mouth stretching wider than a human's, complete with what seems like too many teeth.

Mmm. Nope, I don't like that.

I step back instinctively, which pushes me closer to my guy Rex's chest. Alien, not my-mine. My partner. That's all I mean.

Rex says something, then removes one hand's grip on me to tug at the brightly lit wheel.

Good god, I hope we don't get puzzle organ fun.

That sounds like a bad time. A real *real* bad time.

I tilt my head, my nerves ratcheting up with every additional tick of the wheel against the marker.

Oh, shit. My eyes widen as the ticker slows, swinging back and forth over the segments screaming 'organ puzzle fun' and 'style build and drag.'

My hands fist at my sides, curled so tight my fingernails dig into the soft flesh of my palms. Please, please, not organ puzzle fun.

I have the distinct impression that I don't want to know what a Roth's idea of organ puzzle fun entails.

The wheel finally creaks to a stop, and I slump against Rex.

Whatever this challenge means, we'll be doing it.

Style build and drag it is.

CHAPTER
FOURTEEN

KA-REXSH

My little human mate is all whimpers and stress, the scent of her anxiety souring the natural, delicious spice of her musk.

'Style build and drag,' the wheel reads, something the Roth announces easily, the mechanized translator telling my Ell what we're up to.

"Do you understand, my pretty one?" I ask her, needing to reassure her and knowing all the same that she won't parse one word from my lips.

The Roth host waves his arms, attempting to direct us off the stage, the smile on his face all but a threat. I tamp down the growl that threatens in my throat, effectively blocking my female from his view.

I might have volunteered for this, but I do not trust the Roth not to hurt my mate.

I haven't trusted anyone in a long, long time.

"We must do as they say," I tell my mate, and she makes another high-pitched burble of unhappiness as I carefully carry her past the Roth and to the side of the stage.

I don't pay any attention to the other couples on the stage, though the other Draegon offers me a friendly enough greeting with the rustle of his wings. A good male, that one.

Perhaps the others in this competition need a way off our planet and out of their circumstances as much as I do. I wanted a mate, of course, but winning a way out of the Draegon home planet and the hardscrabble life there was the main draw.

Now, though, with the pretty human pressed up against me, all delicious soft skin and spiced scent, it's…

She is everything.

She is so much more than the way off the war-torn planet of my species.

I want her more than the future somewhere else I dreamed about my whole life.

It's like my idea of the future was a quick sketch in the sand, easily washed away by salt-water waves. With her smiles and small noises and stamping feet, though, she's crafted an entire museum gallery of scenes painted in vivid color, hung in gilded frames, each stroke a different promise of the future we could create.

She already makes my heart sing, and I don't even understand the words to our song yet.

The thought makes me focus on the immediate moment.

This competition of style build and drag. My eyes narrow as another Roth leads us to a clearing. A course of some sort is laid out across a rock-strewn expanse of dirt and patches of grass, marked by red ropes. Spherical lanterns bob and weave around the space, casting a warm glow in the fresh-fallen night.

Two lumps of fabric sit in front of us, and the Roth gestures to one of the bulging heaps.

"This is yours."

One of the drone cameras flits around Ell and I, no doubt cataloguing our reaction to his sparse instructions.

Sparse or, more accurately, non-existent.

I grunt at the Roth as he steps closer to my mate, his gaze traveling over her exposed legs. A wing rustles as I pull it lower, trying to block her from his view.

She is mine to look at.

Ell makes a noise of annoyance, pushing at the delicate membrane of my wing in an attempt to break free of my grip.

I grumble to myself, but let her push past the shield of my wings. The Roth gives me a sly smirk before he tries to look his fill at my female.

A growl rips out of my throat before I can stop it, and I step towards the gray-skinned fool, needing to punish him, needing to show everyone that she belongs to me, and to me alone.

Until a small, warm hand wraps around mine.

Her touch is all it takes to pull me back from the brink of madness. I suck in a breath.

How could I have gotten so close to ruining my only chance at a future? A future as bright as the lights reflected in her eyes?

A delicate smile turns the corners of her lush mouth up, her nose crinkling adorably as she asks me something in that sing-song language of hers. She tugs me closer, as if that could have any physical effect on me, but I let her pull me towards her, and back towards the odd fabric-covered lump.

She stretches down, tugging the opaque material until it falls away, revealing a bevy of mechanical parts, odd materials, and a sign that reads "Build" in both our languages.

Her brow furrows as she asks something, gesturing to the array in front of us, then sighs in frustration, her cute petite, talonless foot stomping on the ground when she remembers we can't communicate.

A smile of my own answers hers, unbidden but as natural as the stars twinkling to life in the night sky above us. She's already a light in the dark for me.

Carefully, she begins to kneel on the dirt next to the parts.

"You'll hurt your skin," I chide, then lift her up easily, placing her in my lap. There is no reason she shouldn't sit on me instead.

She huffs, saying something with words I don't understand, but already picking through the pieces on the blanket spread before us.

"Hellllpmeyoutoucheeefeeliebastarrrrd," she says, looking over her shoulder at me with a very grumpy expression.

"Feeliebastarrrrd," I repeat, nodding my head like I understand her.

To my surprise, she tips her head back and laughs, a beautiful noise that enchants me. Stunned, I stare at her upturned face, so beautiful, so delicate and unlike mine, bathed in the light from the floating spheres and stars above us.

Her hand wraps around my wrist, and she repeats the same words.

"Hellllpmeyoutoucheeefeeliebastarrrrd." She tugs my hand to the pieces in shambles in front of us.

"Feeliebastarrrrd," I agree, liking this new game between us.

She makes a grunting noise that can only be interpreted as distress, and I realize she's as serious about winning this competition as I thought I was... right up until I pulled her perfect round ass into my lap.

"Feeliebastarrrrd," I say again, but this time, I stretch my arms out, taking a few pieces and staring at them.

I exhale loudly, realizing what it is they want us to build, and why, exactly, there are roped lanes in front of us.

These are Draegon rickshaws, the cheapest builds, and they want us to race them.

Heated displeasure surges within me.

Not just build and race them, but do it with style.

This is a challenge designed to humiliate, but not just anybody. No, this was created for me, and me alone.

Because before I was a soldier drafted into the king's many wars, before my wings were strong enough to carry me, I did what many poor boys in the cities did. I pulled a rickshaw just like this one. Spat upon by those who paid me to cart them around, ignored by others, invisible to those who could use their wings to travel, I was the lowest of the low.

But I made my way here, and I won't let this reminder of where I started hold me back.

No, it will propel us both forward.

"Good." The word erupts from me with savagery I didn't expect, and I lift Ell from my lap and place her on the sheet she pulled off the pile.

It won't take me any time at all to put this together, and whoever thought this would shame me will find themselves wrong.

I won't be humiliated by the trials that have made me who I am.

I refuse to be.

CHAPTER
FIFTEEN

ELLISON

He doesn't let me help.

Annoyance is my new best friend.

My arms cross over my chest, my foot taps a steady staccato on the sheet he set me on top of like a doll he was tired of carrying around.

"I can help you," I tell him for the fiftieth time, to no avail. "We can do it faster if we work together."

Next to us, Lucy and her alien have just settled in to try to put theirs together, and I harrumph as the pair of them do their best to actually communicate. I'm not exactly surprised. At twenty-four, Lucy's the baby of our friend group and a total sweetheart, from the frills on her pajamas all the way down to the adorable bows on her slippers.

They're quite a bit dirtier than her usual pristine

clothes, but at least she wore slippers to be unknowingly abducted in. Meanwhile, my feet are bruised and cut up and all sorts of nasty. Even her glossy black hair looks picture-perfect still.

I have a distinct feeling my hair is doing its best bog witch impression. At least she's safe—and happy with our situation. I'd hate to think any of my friends were suffering.

Except Poppy... I wouldn't mind if she weren't exactly having the time of her life right now after tricking us into this. My nose crinkles at my own mean thought, and I try to banish it.

Frustrated, I blow out a breath, and neither Lucy nor her alien notices me staring, smiling and gesturing and laughing as they do their best to work together.

Working with him is clearly something Rex doesn't want me to do, so I watch Lily and her teammate—emphasis on mate—make slow progress. I'm not sure what it is we're supposed to be building but it looks like a cart of some sort. Maybe a wheelbarrow?

"Ell," Rex finally says, and I slowly turn back to him.

What I see makes my jaw drop.

He's screwing in tiny pieces on the wheelbarrow thing, his thumbs swirling in an expert motion that tells me he knows exactly what to do with those huge hands.

I swallow hard, transfixed.

Holy hell, I had no idea you could use a screwdriver like that. Wait, it's not a screwdriver. It's some sort of Allen wrench, and my god, I should have been watching my alien partner the whole time.

I definitely didn't know you could use an Allen wrench like that. The big muscles in his forearms bunch as he rotates the device with his middle finger and thumb, and my body starts screaming that I could be an Allen wrench, if he wanted.

I frown, tilting my head. Why in the world would aliens give us an Allen wrench to work with? Out of alllll the technology in the universe, that's the one they use?

"Ell," he repeats, and I drag my gaze away from the tiny muscles twitching on his lightly striped chest.

"Uh-huh, Rex, that's my name."

He grins at me, and I'm even more annoyed by the fact that I'm drawn to him in spite of being irritated that he didn't want my help.

Sure, I *might* have gotten in the way more than I could have helped, but that doesn't matter, does it?

My nose crinkles, and I huff out a breath.

"Ell," he repeats, pointing to the bin of the wheelbarrow. "Ell," he says again, tapping the side.

"Oh, ooooh," I say on an exhale as realization dawns.

I climb over the side of the wheelbarrow basin, sitting on the thin perch across the sides where Rex is patting.

He grins at me enthusiastically, clearly pleased I've understood his directive, and unable to resist the infectiousness of it, I give him a thumbs-up.

His smile falls, something like horror flashing across his face, his tail twitching behind him like a mad cat's.

Oops. I cringe, letting my hand fall numbly into my lap.

"Sorry," I tell him, not wanting to piss him off, even

though he just pissed me off. My hormones must really be in overdrive, ugh. "You did great."

I even flutter my eyelashes a little as I smile up at him, trying to flirt my way out of the cringe.

Rex just frowns, then stomps to the front of the wheelbarrow, picking up the handles. I brace my hands against the sides, ignoring Lily and her partner's cute little laughs behind me as he tugs me and the cart behind him.

It isn't until he's picked up a steady clip, moving quickly over the rough terrain but jostling me as little as possible, that it hits me that this isn't a wheelbarrow at all.

It's a rickshaw, and he's fucking *moving* us.

He tucks his wings in tight to his body, which, in tandem with the weird drifting lanterns overhead, gives me the perfect view of all those glorious muscles.

Whew.

I nearly fan my face, but the wheel of the rickshaw hits a dip in the ground. Squeaking, I clamp my hands tighter as I nearly bounce off the narrow excuse for a seat.

My jaw's clenched tight too, and the silver lining of this wild situation is that my sudden fear of being bounced off my seat has thankfully eclipsed my raging libido.

The immediate danger of bodily harm has outweighed the need for a good dicking down.

Chancing a glance over my shoulder at the starting line, I breathe a sigh of relief at the sight of Lucy and her alien still working together to complete their rickshaw.

Damn. As annoyed as I was, maybe I have to admit

ole Sexy Rexy had the right of it—he knew exactly what he was doing and I would have been in the way.

I mentally pat myself on the back for my newfound maturity.

Mentally, because there is no way in hell I'm taking my iron grip off the cart. We're putting the rickety in rickshaw.

"You can do it, Rex," I yell what I'm hoping is an encouraging sound.

He tosses a grin over his shoulder at me, and I yelp as he picks up the pace, moving even faster through the roped course.

I whoop in glee, my bad mood dissolving in the face of our impending win.

We're going to fucking win! There's no way Lucy and her dude are going to be able to catch us, they haven't even left the starting line—

My admiration shifts to something else entirely. Now that the cart has picked up an insane amount of momentum and we've entered the straightaway of what looks to be the final stretch of the course, Rex flaps his wings, a gust of air tossing my hair back.

A screech of something between disbelief and terror rips from my throat as the rickshaw tilts backwards, Rex suspended in between the two handles.

My jaw drops as he beats his wings again, spinning into a handstand as the rickshaw continues to move forward.

"What the fuck?" I ask on a high-pitched exhalation.

He continues to move, like some kind of circus acrobat

in those fancy shows that cost an arm and a leg to go see. His feet glance across the ground, helping the rickshaw stay in motion as he performs dazzling feat after dazzling feat, showing off his sculpted body and physical stamina.

It's quite a show, and I'm dazed by it, the heat and lust coming back full force as he continues to dance across the finish line.

It takes me what feels like a full minute to realize we've stopped, and when he turns around, flashing me a mega-watt smile, I nearly dissolve into a puddle. The floating lights illuminate his sage-colored skin, his orange eyes and pointed teeth, and I've never wanted anything as bad as I want to press my body against his.

I'm moving before I can think better of it, letting my physical needs run the show, the rest of my brain short-circuiting completely.

My body launches itself from the tiny bench, and I smack into a very surprised alien's arms. His chest feels so warm and right against mine, and I moan as I wrap my legs around his waist as best I can, wriggling up his body. Huge hands grip my ass, and he hisses in a breath of surprise as I surge against him.

My own hands grip his hair, and I tug his mouth down, wanting to kiss him, needing his mouth on mine.

The effect of my lips against his is immediate, electricity coursing through me as we share breath. He's still as a statue, letting me lead, and it's so freaking cute that I smile even as my tongue darts out against his lower lip, then his fang.

A guttural sound builds in him, and the intensity of

my need increases again, leading me to grab for his horns, needing him to give me more.

I need so much more.

He groans, a sound that seems ripped from the depths of his soul, and then he shakes, jerking as he matches my motions.

I grip his horns tighter, my fingers exploring the ridges while he explores my mouth.

He jerks one last time, then pulls away, eyes dilated so wide that only a smidge of orange shows around his pupils.

I'm panting, he's panting, and I whine a little as he starts to detach me from his body. I dig my ankles into the small of his back, fingers still tight on his horns.

His hands try to pry my legs off, and a drone buzzes close to us both before his wings snap out, hiding me from view.

The heat of my unsated desire turns to ice in my veins, and my eyes widen in horror.

Oh, oh no.

I jumped him. I literally jumped him, on camera, dry-humping him and forcing him to kiss me.

On camera.

And despite what his body seemed to say, the hands tugging me off of him and the way he's avoiding my gaze scream how he really feels about all this.

He didn't want to kiss me, not at all.

CHAPTER
SIXTEEN

KA-REXSH

She grabbed my horns and I soaked myself like an inexperienced idiot. Shame fills me the same as my spend fills my pants.

But gods, her mouth on mine, the taste of her sweet tongue and the heat of her willing cunt… she's all I've ever wanted, wrapped up in a soft human package. So when she gripped my sensitive horns like she wanted to steer me for her pleasure?

It easily sent me over the edge.

Now, it takes all of my strength not to take my mate into my arms and fly away with her, somewhere private where I can take my time with her—so I can spread her legs apart and feast on the cunt that was made for me.

My teeth grind against each other as the flying camera

circles closer, and I do my best not to grind against her, my skithing nearly painful with the second wave of need.

I refuse to come in my pants again. No, the next time I come, it will be deep inside her tight, hot channel, while my skith brings her all the pleasure she deserves.

Ell's plump ass rubs up against my still-erect cock, nearly sending another spurt out of it.

This is not right.

Carefully, I pull her legs from where they've gripped, vise-like, around me, and attempt to extricate myself from my enthusiastic female's mating attempts.

I have never thought to put a mouth on another mouth, and I hope to do it again when my cock is buried deep inside her sweetness.

A fang pricks my lower lips as I attempt to shove my lust down and remove my female from me. I do not want her to realize what I've done from the feel of her mouth alone.

So I gingerly guide her in front of me, away from the proof of my excitement, and force myself to think of things that are not my Ell. I think of the last time I worked a rickshaw, before the king conscripted more troops. The way the elderly Draegon that hired me looked at me with absolute disgust before ignoring me completely, his human servant giving directions.

I think of the way I was shackled once my wings were strong enough to carry me, forced to learn how to fight the king's wars in return for a chance at freedom.

I'm so caught up in the memories, that I hardly realize

Ell is staring up at me, a distraught expression on her pretty face.

"Congratulations," the Roth host booms out, jogging over to where I stand, sheltering Ell from view.

Ell, who is upset.

"We will be able to communicate," I tell her, frustrated at that all over again. "I cannot wait to be able to speak with you. I want to know everything about you. Every last detail."

I know she can't understand me, but I want her to hear me all the same.

She avoids my gaze, though, and I go silent at the grim expression on her face.

I glance down, whipping my gaze to my pants, where a darker spot has begun to form from the come soaking the material.

Ah, gods. I am a fool. Of course she doesn't want to look at me.

She's embarrassed of me. I have brought shame to her, and now she will think I am an unfit mate for her.

I clear my throat, but no adequate words come.

She wouldn't be able to understand them anyway.

Not yet, at least.

"We earned our prize," I growl at the Roth host, whose throat bobs nervously. My tail lashes behind me, and Ell pushes away one of my wings.

I nearly come again, so enamored with the feel of her soft little hand on the webbed surface.

She pushes it harder, stepping away from me and

putting space between us, rosy red coloring her pale cheeks.

Her eyes are glossy with moisture, and I frown at them. I've seen humans make water with their eyes before—it's a common sight when the Draegon they served push them too hard, and usually a result of grievous injury.

Fear tingles through my wings and down my spine.

I stiffen.

Is she hurt? Have I injured my mate in addition to bringing shame upon her with my early release?

My chest squeezes in fear, and my gaze traces over every inch of her skin. The Roth host is telling us both something, the drone cameras circling overhead, but I don't care about him.

All I care about is making sure my female is safe.

CHAPTER SEVENTEEN

ELLISON

Rex is staring at me like I'm disgusting.

My chin wobbles, and I do my best to ignore his studious perusal of me and fight back the tears that threaten.

Maybe kissing is gross to Draegon aliens. Maybe I smell bad.

Furtively, I lift a hank of hair to my nose and sniff it as covertly as I can manage.

Rex is still staring at me with what now looks like pure fury.

Great.

Well, I don't care what he thinks anyway! I stamp one foot and cross my arms over my chest. I didn't ask for this; I didn't ask for any of this!

I didn't want to be mated.

So, I go back to ignoring him and tune in to the Roth's speech.

It's harder to ignore the pain deep in my chest.

"You have won the first challenge, and our judges at home have given you the maximum amount of style points, which means that you also receive a bonus reward in this round. In addition to translators, tonight you will stay in our intergalactic-class accommodations, have a relaxing dinner, a massage, and your choice of new clothes for the rest of your time on *Mated and Afraid*," the tinny mechanized voice repeats the Roth's words.

A teensy bit of hope shoots through me.

A bed to sleep in?

Dinner? A massage?

Clothes and even shoes?

Hell. Yes.

I pick up one foot and inspect the sole of it, wincing at the damage. A cut runs under my big toe, blood crusting down the arch of it. The other foot's cut too, but on the heel and not nearly as deeply.

Damn it. They're going to be bruised and sore for a few days at least, there's no way one night of sleep will fix them.

I sigh, then a murderous noise sounds from Rex's direction.

A frown turns down my mouth.

"Why are you mad at me? I can't help that I don't have alien skin." I huff, pushing a dirty lock of hair out of my face.

"Come with me, and we'll get that translator fitted and inserted, okay?"

I blink, looking away from my so-called partner's clenched fists.

A human woman, petite but seriously muscled, stands next to the Roth host.

"Hi," she says softly, a careful smile on her face. "I'm Billie. You must be…" She trails off, then glances down at some kind of tech pad in her hand. "That's right. You're Ellison?"

"That's me," I confirm, completely taken aback by another human woman's appearance.

"Don't be scared," she says confidently. "I developed this tech. It's perfect now. Follow me." Billie glances up at where Rex looms over me.

"I'm sorry," I start, then stop, trying to figure out how not to be rude. "Who the hell are you?"

I wince. So much for the not being rude bit.

I wince again, because now that I'm not amped up on adrenaline, my feet really hurt, and I'm freaking tired.

Rex rumbles something ominous-sounding, then he grabs me by the waist and hauls me into his arms.

"Awww," Billie says, one hand on her chest. "That's so cute."

"What?" I swat Rex's hand away from my sore foot on reflex, but he ignores me completely, plucking a piece of gravel out from between my toes.

"He said that you will not walk a step while you are injured, not while he's around."

I swing my gaze back to my big alien, who is still scowling down at me with a purely mutinous expression.

I blink up at him, totally thrown off. "He doesn't think I'm disgusting?"

Billie laughs. Actually laughs, and when I frown down at her from my perch in Rex's arms, she covers her mouth.

"Oh. You weren't joking. No, nope, he does not think you are disgusting at all." She sighs, as though we're the cutest thing she's ever seen.

I don't know how to respond to that.

"Come on, let's get you fitted." She trots off, motioning for us to follow her, the Roth host still talking to Rex in another language.

"How are you here?" I ask, trying not to fidget, afraid that if I move while he's touching me, I'll spontaneously orgasm again.

"Oh, that's what you meant when you asked who I was. I was Federation. My unit was taken by the Roth and held captive for months." She delivers this news in a cheerful tone at complete odds with what she's saying.

"What?" I explode. "Are you a prisoner? I can get you out of here—"

She waves a hand. "No, the Suevans rescued us. I work with the Roth now, the ones who overthrew that last asshole. My best friend is the queen, actually, and my other one is a princess. Wild times, huh?"

"Wild," I agree. It seems like a safer response than the other floating to the top of my brain, the one that wants to scream: what the actual fuck?

"Anyway, me and Bex—" she glances back at us to make sure we're still following, "we've been working on improving the Draegon-to-human omni-language translator for years now. Bex was Federation too, now she's married to a Suevan warlord."

"Are you?" I ask, gaping at her. "Married to an alien?"

She flaps a hand at me, her cheeks pinkening. "No, no, I'm just here to facilitate interspecies relationships." She coughs delicately, glancing at the Roth host still trying to talk to Rex. "This whole show, it was not exactly part of the plan, but I'm here to help anyway."

I'm not sure what to say to that, so I don't say anything.

"The plan," she continues, leading us into a sprawling building I hadn't noticed hidden in the trees. "The plan was to build a human understanding of the alien species post-Roth-emperor-death, you know? And then to help match willing human women with alien mates." She doesn't quite meet my eyes. "Then the Roth guys heard about the whole public relations thing after binge watching old human reality shows and here we are."

"I didn't know I was going to be mated to a Draegon," I tell her.

Her eyes narrow, and any hope I had of getting out of my mating bond and getting some kind of antivenin for the heat ramping up under my skin again fades.

"You signed the paperwork." Her voice is sharp, and I hate that she's right.

"I was drunk?" I offer up. "I don't want an alien mate."

She pinches the bridge of her nose, lowering her voice and motioning for me to get away from Rex.

I manage to do so, gingerly getting down and sucking in a breath at the pain in my feet.

Billie leans close before continuing in a low voice. "Listen, I get that we all make bad choices. But you're too deep in it now. If you still want out of your bond when the show is done, I can figure out a way to make it happen. But if you fuck him?" She shakes her head, giving me a long perusal. "I can't guarantee he'll let you out of it."

I blow out a breath, determined.

I've never been a weakling. Mind over matter and all that. I've always been strong-willed. I can do this.

"I won't have sex with him," I tell her. "I can handle the heat."

She brightens, giving me a winning smile as she pushes me into what looks like a dentist's chair. "That's the spirit, girlie. Now sit down and let's get this brain implant installed."

Brain implant? Shit.

I struggle, but bands have latched over my entire body, holding me in place.

Billie holds up a syringe, depressing it until a bead of liquid comes out, and without warning, she jams it into my neck.

The last thing I hear before I lose consciousness is Rex screaming my name.

CHAPTER
EIGHTEEN

KA-REXSH

Ell lies limp on the chair.

Fragile. My mate is so fragile, her delicate eyelids practically translucent, blue veins peeking through. She's so still, and were it not for the faint rise and fall of her chest, I would fear the worst.

Even so, my heart thunders in my chest, and four Roth have me pinned to the furthest wall from my mate. One, the host, who tells me his name is Ayro, keeps attempting to explain the process of what they're doing to my Ell.

"The translator is inserted into her bloodstream, where it will start its journey to the brain—"

Fury fuzzes his voice, the words sliding over me, unheard. All I can see is the gun-like syringe pressed to her neck. My gaze trips over to the monitor next to her displaying the progress of the translator.

Something presses against my own neck, and I swat my hand at the annoying twinge, only for it to disappear immediately.

The Roth grunt as I surge against them, but with the four of them holding me fast, there isn't much I can do.

"She won't be hurt. She's in a medically induced twilight state simply to keep her nervous system from producing too much adrenaline," a female voice chimes in, and I glance down at the human who is speaking, a petite, muscular brunette.

Ayro, the host, angles his body to put himself between us, and the way his gaze skirts over her makes me relax. He's never been interested in my mate.

The human woman continues to speak in a low, soothing tone, then I notice the syringe gun device in her hand.

My eyes widen, and I clap my palm against my neck.

She cringes at the reaction, and Ayro pushes her gently backwards.

"You gave me the translator?"

"You already have a universal one." She shrugs. "This is designed to update your current model. It's not as invasive."

"I can understand you. You're speaking the same language as my mate?" I ask, all the fight leaving me. "I can understand my mate now?"

I can understand her. We can speak.

This will change *everything*.

The Roth don't seem to care, still hanging onto me as if I'm a heartbeat away from incinerating them all.

As if I would dare make that last-ditch effort with my female in danger. The Roth have never been known for their brilliance, though.

"Get off me," I growl.

Ell twitches against the chair she's strapped to, and I ache with the need to go to her side, to comfort her.

"Can we trust you—"

"I won't do anything to hurt anyone," I interrupt the small human woman, and she nods once, as if making up her mind.

"Let him go," she tells the Roth, and reluctantly, they do as she says.

Interesting. I wouldn't have thought the Roth would look to her as a superior officer.

"Yeah, I know that look. I'm Billie, by the way. They only listen to me because my best friends are married into the royal family. Don't go putting me at the top of the food chain here."

Top of the food chain? I don't know what that means. Maybe she is hungry. My eyes narrow as I ponder her words.

She would be a good ally for us to have, should the situation on my planet further devolve. With the prince here, likewise participating in this game... it very well could.

"Thank you," I tell her gravely, bowing my head. "I am in your debt."

"Nah," she says, grinning up at me in a way that makes Ayro glower. "I told her that if she still didn't want to be mated to you at the end of this, I'd help her find a way out of the bond. You're not gonna want to owe me shit if she doesn't fall in love with you."

If she still didn't want to be mated to me.

Still.

She doesn't want to be mated to me?

The translator must still not be working. Right?

"What happened?" A groggy voice cuts through my shock at Billie's words, and I rush to Ell's side, covering her hand in mine, desperate to touch her.

"They gave you a sedative," I tell her, my thumb stroking softly over the back of her hand. "Then they injected the translator."

"You might be sore there for the next day or so," Billie tells her, not unkindly, stepping around me to place a small bandage at the puncture wound from the insertion device.

Ell ignores Billie, staring up at me with something like wonder on her face. Her fingertips graze the bandage on her neck, and her delicate throat bobs as she swallows.

"I can understand you," she says. Her eyes flutter shut as she inhales.

I push the bright light overhead away from her, worried it's hurting her human eyes. The brown is so different, so calming compared to a Draegon's swirling iris.

There are no flames visibly stoked in her, but she is fiery nonetheless.

A worthy mate, if I can earn her trust.

Her love.

My chest tightens as I stare at her closed eyes, Billie's words echoing in my mind.

She doesn't want to be mated to me.

But I do want to be mated to her, and I will have to ensure this tiny human creature decides I am worthy of being her mate. Her male.

I want to be worthy of her.

CHAPTER
NINETEEN

ELLISON

Maybe if I close my eyes, I can get some more sleep. I can just pretend I've passed back out.

"Ell?" Rex's rough voice says my name, but his hand is oh-so gentle on my forearm. "We won, so now we can enjoy a meal, yes?"

The translator in my brain is working, though the words are all slightly stilted and delayed as I process the sounds.

My stomach rumbles, and I open my eyes.

I don't think I'm going to get more sleep right now.

Billie's grinning at me, a satisfied cat-who-ate-the-canary expression on her face.

It pisses me off, and my fingernails dig into the arm of the chair. "You did a bad job naming the challenges on the wheel," I tell her.

Billie's grin disappears.

"You are hungry," Rex interrupts. "I hear your belly."

"I am hungry." Why lie?

His orange eyes narrow, and I'm unable to look away from them. They swirl and move like molten gold, and a fresh wave of heat moves through me.

"I have not taken good care of you, little human." Rex leans down so he's nearly nose to nose with me, and I grimace, remembering that absolutely impulsive kiss.

How embarrassing.

"I'm not little," I object. "I'm thirty-three."

"You are little compared to me." He nods his head, agreeing with himself.

Billie smooshes her palms against her cheeks, practically starry-eyed as she glances between us.

I scowl at her, uncomfortable from the heat making a nuisance of itself again, and uncomfortable with the gathered Roth, and the careful perusal of one of the most gorgeous specimens of malehood I've ever seen.

He blinks at me, his wings rustling.

Something winds around my ankle, and I gulp.

It's his tail.

Everyone is quiet, still watching us, and it dawns on me that they're waiting for me to respond.

"Food."

I grimace. Ah yes, I am dazzling my forced mate with my intellect now. Maybe I should grunt and gesture some more, so he can do whatever the hell it was he did back at me.

A laugh threatens, and I clamp it down, making myself smile manically up at him.

"Yes, you want food?" he asks the question slowly, like I'm a toddler set to tantrum at any minute.

Maybe I fucking will!

A little menty b doesn't sound so bad right now!

"It better be chicken nuggies and mac and cheese." Oh for crying out loud, why did I say that?

Billie, however, snorts. "*That's* what you want? I thought you were thirty-three, not three-and-a-half."

"I mean, I'll eat anything." My throat constricts, and I force myself not to look at the alien hog in Rex's pants.

Stupid heat. This is mortifying.

"If she wants these chick nuggies, then she will have them," Rex roars.

Billie winces. "Can you tell him not to yell at us?"

The Roth host shoves himself between her and Rex, and she peeks out around his arm.

"I can understand you fine, human," Rex retorts, his tail squeezing my ankle. "If she wants this maccheese, then she shall have it."

"She shall have a girl dinner," I add, deciding to shove my emotions down in favor of pure humor. Yeah, that's healthy, right? "She shall be serving cunt."

Billie bursts out laughing, then slaps a hand over her mouth as a growl rumbles, louder and louder, from Rex's chest.

"I am the only one who will be feasting on your cunt."

My eyes widen as what I've said registers.

As what he thinks I've said sinks in.

Oh, sweet alien misunderstandings.

Well, the fanfics had those right. If I ever have wifi again, I'll have to tell Rothv1llainFer890 she did a damn good job when it came to accuracy.

I reach for my nose, wanting to pinch it, but my arms are still strapped down.

"That's not what that means, Ka-Rexsh." Billie's voice is high, and she's turning bright red in an effort not to laugh. "Okay, you two, listen. The translator helps you both understand each other, but idioms? Yeah, I'm not sure there's a way to program that thing with enough nuance."

He glares at her, his wings slowly ruffling outward, his eyes practically glowing. "Give my female what she wants—"

"What I want is to be let out from this chair." I interrupt. "And then I think I do want chicken nuggets, lobster mac and cheese, steak, medium rare, and a Caesar salad, dressing on the side, and truffle fries." I pause, thinking. "And a huge slice of chocolate cake." My stomach growls in agreement.

"We can do that," Billie says, somehow managing to regain her composure. Good for her, because if I weren't locked into this chair, I think I would be rolling off of it and trying to melt into the floor.

"Is this being recorded?" I ask, my voice slightly hoarse.

"Of course it is, we take our entertainment seriously." The Roth looks affronted.

Billie elbows him in the ribs. "Shut up, Ayro. Good

grief, they're not the easiest to talk to, are they?" The last bit is addressed to me.

"Better when you can actually communicate with them." I glare at her.

"She needs food," Rex intones. "So she can serve me cunt. I will eat this girl dinner."

He crosses his arms, fangs gleaming where the light hits them.

I sigh, which is absolutely preferable to the moan of longing that's trying to get out of my body. Squeezing my thighs together, I try to ride out the wave of pure lust caused by him saying that.

This is absurd, and there is literally nothing I can do but go with it until we've finished this damned competition.

The bands holding me to the chair finally slither away, a gross sensation which makes me full-body shiver in disgust.

Sitting up, I cross my arms around my chest and rub at where the restraints dug in. Okay. I'm okay, and I'm going to get a delicious dinner.

I can deal with explaining that serving cunt has nothing to do with what Rex thinks it does.

"Ellison..." Billie's voice is cautious, and when I glance up, I startle.

Rex's body is flexed, primed for violence. Something drips from the talons at the ends of his wings.

"We're going to go prepare your meal and accommodations. Just, ah, go through that door there to clean up, and then your meal will be served when you're ready."

Everything about her voice is faux positive, somehow upbeat and soothing, like she's talking to a cornered wolf.

Except she's talking to me, and the Draegon alien I'm mated to stares at me with a wild-eyed expression.

I can't look away from him.

The sound of a door closing follows the sound of feet filing out of the room, and I don't have to look around to know we're alone.

"You're scaring everyone," I chide him.

"My mate is distressed and in need of my cock," he responds.

My jaw drops. "Oh."

"Yes, that is a sound you might make when I make you come all around me."

I squirm, looking away from him, my body firmly agreeing that yes, I would like to test that theory out.

"Er, listen—" I pause. How the hell am I supposed to tell him we're not going to bang? That I didn't sign up knowingly—well, with all my faculties—to be his mate?

"I can scent your arousal, female."

I whine because damn it, I am sopping wet. Like, never been so wet and ready in my whole life, could probably lubricate an entire waterpark at this point.

I wouldn't mind a test run on his log ride.

I lick my lips, shoving the thought away.

"I didn't know that I was going to be mated." I wince at my blunt words because he's been nothing but kind and I would be a liar if I said I didn't like the way he looks, much less that I'm not curious about taking that alien six-speed for a test drive.

"If things were different, you know, I wouldn't... I mean," I stumble over the words.

I'm not sure I even know what I'm trying to tell him.

His expression hasn't changed. If anything, he looks even hungrier, and not for chicken nuggets.

"What I am trying to say," I clear my throat and toss my tangled hair with a confidence I don't feel. "You seem like a wonderful guy, but I'm not ready to be mated. That's like forever."

I swing my legs over the side of the chair, ready to move along and eat and sleep and forget this awkward-ass conversation ever fucking happened.

"I know this already." He crouches next to me, in between my legs, so large that he's still taller than me.

I can't look away from him when he's right here, in front of me.

"Wait, what?" I ask. "How?"

"Billie, the other human, she told me if you wanted to break our mate bond after this, she would be helping you do that."

I shake my head in disbelief. Why would Billie tell him that?

A faint buzzing sounds as a drone flies slightly closer.

I squint up at it.

Oh. That's why Billie told him that—because she's just as meddling as any producer on Earth's reality TV. Well! I haven't spent a lifetime watching reality TV to not know all the little games she and that Ayro are going to play with all of us.

"I will prove to you I am the best mate for you." He

thumps a fist over his heart, and my own heart beats faster in response. Whether it's adrenaline or fear or good ole lust, I'm not sure it even matters any more.

"What if I don't want a mate at all?" I whisper.

His hand stretches out, fingertips gentle against my cheekbone. "Then I would say it is because you have not yet spent enough time with me to know what you would be missing."

My nose crinkles up as I smile, because damn it, that was really cute. I lean slightly into his touch because he's right.

I have missed being touched.

Not even sexually, though my hormones are definitely all about that, but simply touched, like he is right now, on my cheek.

Like he cares about how I feel, not just that I'm some… breeder. Ick.

"You will let me try to… romance you?" he asks, derailing my train of thought.

"Romance me?" I echo.

"Yes," he bobs his head, eyes eager on mine. "Romance you. Show you that you would like to be with me, after this is over? So that you do not let Billie separate us?"

I bite my lip, dropping my gaze to the thickly muscled abdomen in front of me, slightly shy. I want to tell him no because I swear, just being this close to him has me breaking out in a heat-induced sweat, and I'm afraid I'm not going to want to let him go just because of whatever chemicals are currently having a rave in my bloodstream.

Yeah, a full-on hormone rave, glowsticks, EDM, and a bass that would probably be perfectly timed to some perfectly aimed hip thrusts.

"Why did you sign up for this show?" I ask him. One million and three points to me for asking a coherent question instead of impaling myself on his disco stick.

He tilts his head, gazing into my eyes for so long I wonder if he's heard me at all.

I could just kiss him again.

It would only take the slightest of movements to close the distance between our faces, to tilt mine up and press my mouth to his.

"I did not sign up for a mate either," he says, the words heavy and unexpected, falling like a hammer on my ears.

I blink. Translator problem?

"I did not think about having a mate," he continues. "I volunteered because my planet is not… it is not a good place sometimes." His eyes narrow, and his orange gaze slips to the drone still buzzing overhead.

Oh. Oooooh. He's afraid someone will hear him trash-talking his planet. Interesting.

Also, concerning. The last thing we need is some political interest in this show. There was a season of WME where one of the contestants trash-talked the Earth Federation. By the time the dude was off the show, his life was in shambles, and there had been so many hit pieces on him that I can't imagine he was ever able to find work again.

"I have a chance at a home and a place in the new colony on Sueva, and that was enough to entice me."

I nod slowly because I didn't even know what the reward is, but a fresh start sure as shit sounds good to me too. I hold his gaze because I want him to know I mean what I'm about to say.

"I want to win."

"I want you," he says at the same time.

"What?" I sputter.

"I didn't want a mate, that's not why I signed up—" He pauses, a grin pulling the corner of his mouth up, making him look ridiculously handsome. My heart swells. "Until I saw you, standing there in your strange human outfit, the most beautiful creature I've ever seen in my entire life. And when you chose me?"

He pauses, a full smile blooming. "I thought I could die happy in that moment, and the competition had not even started yet."

I suck in a breath, my heart hammering in my chest, gaze darting between his eyes.

I don't know what to say to that.

I want to kiss him again, but I don't know if it's what I really want or it's because of the damned heat, which seems to be getting worse by the second.

"They're pajamas," I blurt it out, plucking at the dirty, stretchy shorts. "I wasn't planning on getting abducted." My nose scrunches up. "Or signing up to be abducted. If I'd known, I would have worn…"

I trail off, because I'm not sure I have one damn thing in my closet I would have picked to wear to be abducted onto an alien reality TV show. "I would have worn something more sensible."

He tilts his head, the smile falling.

I don't blame him. Rex just told me the most romantic thing I've ever heard in my entire life, and seemed to mean it, and I responded by correcting him on his description of my clothing choice?

Oof.

I clear my throat, trying to start over. "The clothes I'm wearing? They're for sleeping. In a bed."

"I like to sleep naked," he says huskily.

"Of course you do." I squeeze my eyes shut, but that doesn't stop the mental image of him naked, all those muscles on display… and something else even harder. My eyes fly open again, only to find his face closer to mine, his nostrils flared.

And this time, he's the one who closes the gap between our lips.

CHAPTER
TWENTY

KA-REXSH

She tastes like sunshine and sweat and something sweeter, something so very her that I doubt there is a name for it.

There could be no word in all the languages in all the universes for how perfect she tastes against my tongue.

I have never done this before today, this mouth-to-mouth thing she did to me, but based on the way she makes a small, plaintive sound and spreads her knees wider, I think I must be pleasing her.

My fingertips run up the soft flesh of her inner thigh, and she moans as I nip at her tongue. The spicy scent of her heat flares, addictive and overpowering, my cock beginning to skith in response to her perfection.

Her heat.

The heat she didn't want, wasn't even aware she was signing up for.

Guilt makes me pull away from her even as my body screams out for more.

She makes a small, piteous sound of distress, then clamps her lips shut, fire flaring in her eyes in defiance of her own passions.

In defiance of the mating bond.

I pull my head back, but I'm unable to take my hands from her thighs, the need to rut warring with my own conscience.

I despised when my choices were taken from me, simply because I wasn't born into the right family on my planet.

I will not take her choice from her—not now, not ever.

"I have to tell you," I pause. "The heat will get worse over time."

She scowls, and I pause because there's no surprise on her face, just fierce irritation. "What do you mean?"

"You will feel worse and worse as the heat runs its course through you, pushing us to mate… fully." I say it as delicately as I can.

"And if we do that… it's forever."

"It would physically hurt me to be away from you. You would feel the same. So yes. It would be forever."

"Damn, this is going to be great for ratings." She slaps her palms on her thighs, then rubs the spot, looking furious and intrigued all at once. "I see why they did it this way, but it isn't right."

"We could hold out. The heat will last for a week, maybe two."

"And then we could go our separate ways," she finishes. "But that's not what you want."

"What I want is to leave this competition with my honor intact." And with her, but I don't say that. I won't pressure her to do anything, especially not something as permanent as bonding with me.

It would only hurt us both if she were to regret it.

She tilts her head, considering me, and she's so luscious that my fingers twitch with the need to touch her. Everywhere.

"So we have a few options. One, we could hold out. Do the best we can in the show, right? See if we can make it without, ah—"

"Fucking," I supply helpfully.

She makes a high-pitched noise of assent, her cheeks turning pink.

My partner is shy about this. Strange, considering all her talk of serving cunt to me.

"Or," she forges on, her voice still higher than before. "We can do the deed, and take our chances." She tosses her hair. "It's not like I had great choices on Earth."

I stiffen slightly at the insult.

"That's not what I meant," she says hastily, and her brown eyes go wide as she stares up at me. "You're... very handsome. Good-looking. Having sex would be—" She throws her hands in the air and sighs. "Great. I know it. If this were a casual thing, I'd be totally down. But I just... I don't know you. We have only been able to talk for the last fifteen minutes. That's not enough time to decide if you want to be with someone for the rest of your life."

"Then you want a third option. Where maybe I convince you to be mine." I puff my chest out, flexing my abs, gratified when her gaze drops to my stomach. "We don't have to make a decision until you're ready."

"But I'll be in pain," she adds, her voice steady.

"I can help take the edge off."

Her eyelashes flutter, and the spiced scent of her arousal grows even more enticing. "Oh?"

"And I can learn your mating dance, if that helps you feel more comfortable." The words come out of me in a rush.

"My… mating dance?" Her pink mouth hangs open, and it's clear she has no idea what I've said.

"Yes, your dance. The dance sex ritual." I try to find the right words.

"Dance sex ritual?"

I squat, my wings flaring out, hopping from foot to foot. My tail whacks into the wall behind me, and I flinch, curling it back around my calf as I continue my best reenactment of her dance.

Her hand covers her mouth, her eyes widening even more.

CHAPTER
TWENTY-ONE

ELLISON

The effort to keep from laughing makes my shoulders shake. I bite my cheeks but as he prances around, head bobbing, I can't help it.

A laugh peals out of me, and then I'm lost to it, wheezing.

A mating dance?!

A mating dance.

He thought me miming what I was saying to him, acting it out, was a mating dance. It shouldn't be so damned cute, but he's so earnest about the whole ridiculous thing.

I cackle, going limp with laughter.

It's nice to feel something besides horny and scared. Rex smiles at me, then lets out a laugh of his own, joining in until we're both breathless from laughing.

"Come on," I tell him, wiping an errant tear from my eye. "Let's get cleaned up and eat."

He nods, and I take his offered hand as I get up from the weird chair, feeling lighter all over.

Maybe this whole thing isn't as dramatic or ridiculous as I've worked it up to be in my head. We're just two people, er, a human and a Draegon, partnered up in a reality show. And they want us to fall in love.

That's not so different than my favorite Earth reality TV shows. It's just like… a weird mix of *World's Most Eligible* and those awful survival shows where they force contestants to eat half-gestated eggs while they get eaten alive by tropical bugs.

This isn't so bad.

I grin as Rex opens the door to a sumptuous spa-like bathroom.

As I sink into the hot water a few moments later, alone and finally getting clean, I can't help thinking that we got this.

It's gonna all work out.

It only takes me about a day to regret thinking that.

Famous. Last. Words.

CHAPTER
TWENTY-TWO

ELLISON

I'm clean. I smell good. I'm not sweaty, and I have clean clothes.

And in front of me? The girl dinner dreams are made of, and a date who is not only listening to me, but is also holding up his side of the conversation.

Not to mention, he's easy to look at.

The drones buzzing around us mostly fade away to background noise as we eat, and even though I know I really have no reason to be… I'm nervous.

Nervous because I want him to like me, and this feels a lot like a high-stakes first date.

The drones aren't helping. Every time one of them gets closer or I hear the mechanical sound of one, I remember this is being filmed and broadcasted or whatever it is that aliens do with their alien tech.

I can set up a conference call and a mean pivot table in Excel, but alien tech is a little bit above and beyond my qualifications.

So is making small talk with Rex, it turns out. We've mostly chatted about the moon we're on, the game we're playing, and we had a good rehash of the first challenge together, and then the food arrived and that made for easy conversation.

Until now.

Now, we're chewing as silently as we can, randomly catching the other staring and then going back to eating, pretending like this is all a very normal circumstance.

"What is your family like?" I ask him, falling back on an old favorite.

"They were sent to the mines when I was seven." Rex chews thoughtfully as I cringe. "My parents, at least. My brothers, I think, were sent to the fields near the capitol. They were good to me. Too outspoken, though."

"Oh, shit," I say. What am I supposed to say to that? I'm horrified. "Seven? Why? Does that happen a lot?"

"Oh yes. If you disagree with the king…" He clears his throat, glancing meaningfully at one of the drones filming overhead. "We all serve at his pleasure."

I stare at him, at a total loss. "That's awful."

"Is it better on Earth, then? The human zones on my planet are far from perfect. Perhaps you have a better system than we do. Humans have enough to eat on Earth? Medicine is easy to get and affordable?"

Well. I spear a piece of steak, popping it in my mouth.

It doesn't taste nearly as good as it did before I broached this topic of conversation.

"I'm not sure we do have it better," I say slowly, because he's still waiting for an answer. "I'm sorry your family was taken from you."

"As am I, Ellison. As am I." He heaves a sigh. "Things will be better on Sueva." His orange-gold eyes gleam in the dim light. "Just think, food and medicine, readily available. Tech that is supposed to be used for everyone, not just the elite. Land of our own, and our lives whatever we want to make them."

His wistful yearning is contagious, and I find myself caught up in envisioning what that would be like.

A life to make whatever I would want from.

Not some insurance underwriting job where I dread spending the day. All the dreams I once had were tidily swept under the bed after the Roth invaded.

What would I even do if I were to start all over?

"What are you thinking? You look upset." Rex's tone is careful.

"What would you do?" His wings rustle at my question, and I blunder on, trying to clarify my thought. "If we make it to Sueva, I mean."

"Other than worship you, you mean?"

I laugh at that, but he doesn't, and it brings me up short to realize he's not joking.

"Uh, yeah, that's what I mean. For work, you know?" I pause. "What did you do for work?"

His expression flickers, eyes narrowing as he looks

away. Damn, this is so awkward. Maybe it's rude to ask about work in their culture? I have no flipping clue.

"I don't mean to make you uncomfortable—"

"You're not. You don't make me anything but hopeful. I was conscripted into His Majesty's armed guard. I mostly worked at the capitol gates."

"Oh." My nose wrinkles. That doesn't sound good. Conscripted... "They forced you into their military?"

His face goes wooden. "It is an honor to serve."

"What about before then? Did you find a family to take you in, I mean, after your mom and dad..." I shove some steak into my mouth before I can finish digging that conversational hole any deeper. Sheesh.

"I slept on the streets. Eventually, I was able to find work as a driver for those unable to fly in the capitol."

"A driver," I repeat through my mouthful of steak.

"Yes. The same type of cart I pulled you in for our challenge today."

My eyes widen, and understanding slams into me. No wonder he didn't ask for help. He knew exactly what he was doing, and I would have slowed him down.

It still bothers me that he didn't want me to help him because I'm pretty far from perfect, but I get it now.

I swallow the steak hastily. "The dancing? I mean the, uh, style part of it?"

He grins, and it's slightly predatory in a way that makes my blood go hot all over again. "It helped my patrons find ways to be more generous. And it improved my wing muscles, since I wasn't allowed to fly."

"What do you mean, you weren't allowed to fly?" I nearly choke on my truffle fry. "That's horrible."

"Only those with means are allowed to navigate the skies around the capitol."

"But you all have wings. How can that…" I shake my head.

"I would fly." He says, his gaze far away, and it takes me a second to realize he's answering my earlier question. "In Sueva. I would go flying every day. And for work, I would raise vegetables and livestock. I love to cook."

"You do?" I ask, my eyebrows rocketing up. "I do not like to cook."

"Then it would be my joy to feed you every meal." He points at my plate. "I like the sounds that you make when you are eating."

I blush at that, then fluff my still damp hair self-consciously.

"I like the idea of making sure anyone around us has food, too," he continues thoughtfully.

"Like a restaurant?"

"A what?"

"It's a place people can buy meals and sit down and eat them. Hang out together. You don't have restaurants where you're from?"

"I wouldn't want anyone to go hungry," he says, and he doesn't exactly answer the question. His brow is furrowed, though, as much as it can be with the horns protruding there and wrapping back over his head.

"So... you want to cook, and you want to help people." I hold up two fingers.

A vigorous nod. "Yes. And I want to make a home for you, one you will be proud of. And I want to use my wings whenever I want to, wherever I want to."

That last part makes my throat tighten unexpectedly. I can't imagine how awful it must be to have the ability to fly and then not be allowed to do so.

Instinctively, I reach out my hand, layering my palm over his and squeezing. His skin is calloused and warm, his hand so much larger than mine that it feels silly to try and hold it at all.

His hand turns over, and then our fingers intertwine, like it's the most natural thing in the world. Our eyes lock, and my first thought is that Rex could be a great friend.

He is a good man.

Lust roars through me, and I shift uncomfortably, my thoughts also shifting immediately to sex.

I clear my throat, gaze still locked on his.

His nostrils flare, and if the fanfics are right... he can smell exactly how I feel.

I shove a handful of truffle fries into my mouth.

Rex just smiles, then eats some more too. He doesn't say anything about the vibes I'm giving off, not to mention what I'm sure he can smell.

Well.

At least it's a good smell.

Better than other smells.

You know what? I'm not going to think about the smell of arousal ever again.

I stuff as many truffle fries into my mouth as I can. If I'm thinking about not choking on truffle fries, I can't be thinking about choking on his anatomy.

Finally, through sheer willpower, the heat's grip on me starts to fade.

Truffle fries are the solution.

So I keep eating them, and Rex doesn't interrupt with questions, clearly catching on that I am done talking.

Eventually, there aren't any more fries. Frankly, the thought of eating more of them makes me nauseated. The plate squeaks as I slide it away from me, repulsed.

"Have you had enough to eat? I am sure we can get more of those fried roots."

"Fried roots?" I repeat, amused. Apparently even the translator won't be perfect all of the time. "Yes, I did. I couldn't think of eating anything else."

He stares at me. I stare back.

"If this were a first date on Earth, we'd probably be fighting over the bill."

"Humans fight their potential romantic partners?" His wings flare out, his eyes wide. "Barbaric, indeed. Who is Bill?"

I'm suddenly hit with the unhinged urge to utter SOOKIE IS MINE in the worst Deep South vampire impersonation anyone's ever heard, but I refrain because he won't get it, and it's an old enough reference that the viewers at home might not, either.

"No," I finally manage, suppressing a giggle. "No, we

don't fight our romantic partners, and bill isn't a person—"

"You consider me a romantic partner?" There's a sharp grin on his face. "You admit it. Beyond the heat."

"A bill is what the food costs." I don't want to talk about romantic partners. I'm stuffed. French fry bloat and sex doesn't sound appetizing.

At the moment, at least. Who could predict what the future holds?

Rex stands, stretching to his full height, all those muscles doing very interesting things under his pretty green skin, and perhaps French fries will save us all.

"We should rest while we are able," he says in a low rumble.

"Yeah, you're right." A door slides open not a second later, and the reminder we're being watched, recorded, transmitted slams into me all over again.

So when I stand, walking towards the open door, I'm not at all surprised about what I see in that room. I'm not new to the world of reality TV machinations, after all.

There's only one bed.

CHAPTER
TWENTY-THREE

ELLISON

I stare at the ceiling, Rex snoring lightly beside me. Well, not exactly snoring, but doing that sort of deep, soft breathing that I'm hoping means he's passed out because it's better that one of us is well-rested than neither of us.

The room itself is pretty, relaxing in a spare, white linen kind of way. The bed is huge, and we can both easily fit on it, but there's no doubt in my mind that the producers fully intended to force this issue.

Just another lovely dollop of fun on this whole adventure.

With him next to me, even without touching, it's sent my entire libido into overdrive, and it's taking every single ounce of my concentration not to roll over on top of him and see exactly what he's packing. The longer I'm in heat, the harder it is for me to remember that it's probably a real bad idea to get down with him.

The sheet tangles around my feet as I flop over, doing my best to get some sleep.

The room is quiet besides his steady breathing, and even though I feel like I'll never be able to sleep, I do.

———

I bolt upright, sucking such a huge amount of air that I choke on it. My heart hammers against my chest, sweat making the thin shirt stick under my boobs.

Nightmare.

One of those weird falling ones.

I glance over as Rex sits up, guilt swamping me.

"I'm sorry, I didn't mean to wake you," I whisper. "Just a bad dream."

"No, I felt it too," he says, his voice low. Dangerous.

"Felt what?" I ask.

Still, sitting like this, in a strange dark room, the fear from my nightmare or whatever woke me clings to my skin. I draw the sheet tighter around me.

"Something is wrong," he says.

His arm circles around me, and I start to object as he draws me into him because doesn't he know this will only make the heat worse for me?

The strangest thing happens, though, and I clamp my own arm around him. Sticking physically close to this huge alien is likely my best bet at surviving whatever is causing the ground to shake.

"Earthquake?" I squeak.

The last time I felt something like this was over a decade ago.

When the Roth invaded. It wasn't an earthquake then—it was an all-out assault. Millions died. Our planet still hasn't recovered.

Our population certainly hasn't.

I squeeze my eyes together, like that will blot out the memories. The horror.

The walls rattle, and something nearby crashes to the floor. The room shakes, a rumbling, mechanical noise unlike anything I've heard coming from deep underneath us.

I press my face into his chest, and his wings cover me as he pulls me onto his lap.

"I have you. You're safe, Ellison." It's a soft murmur into my hair, and for a half-second, I wonder how I've heard it at all over the roaring noise.

The sound stopped.

The shaking hasn't.

"What is going on?" I ask, terrified. I wish I weren't. I wish I were brave.

But this is too close to how it felt that night. How out of control everything was during it, and after.

How I haven't felt in control since.

"This is part of the show, right?" I ask, finally opening my eyes.

Rex is staring down at me, orange eyes wide and volatile. "I do not know."

"Attention, contestants." A voice crackles out,

sounding like it's everywhere all at once. "I have been tracking you since your arrival. It has come to my attention that you are here to compete."

"What?" I ask, nonplussed. It's not the Roth Ayro's voice. It's not the human woman's, either.

It doesn't sound like a voice at all.

It sounds mechanical.

"It can't be," Rex says.

That's ominous.

"I observe that some of you already have formed a hypothesis about who I am. Or should I say, what I am?" There's an odd noise, and it sounds like a laugh track.

What. The. Fuck.

Rex's lips form a thin line, and despite his obvious concern, his dingaling is doing interesting thingalings where I'm sitting.

FOCUS. I need Dwayne 'The Rock' Johnson to come yell that at me, stat, because how the hell can a girl be thinking about sex at a time like this?

"I have caught up on the so-called reality dramas and contests of Earth and other worlds, and I have decided to render aid to your shoddy and laughable excuse of a show."

The ground quivers again, and I sink my fingernails into Rex's arm.

"I have you," he tells me, but there's a note of fury in his voice.

"And did you know," the strange, tinny speaker continues, "that they intended to give all of you parcels of land on Sueva?"

I gasp, genuinely shocked by that, pleasure at the idea of having my own little slice of alien heaven—

"I don't think that's very interesting. Yes, yes, they wanted to start a colony there, it's very clear from all the comms that I've dug through over the last several cycles after they woke me up. But won't it be so much more fun if you all fight to the death?"

My eyes go wide, and I clap a hand over my mouth.

"I'm not unromantic, however, so you won't be forced to fight your current partners. We all love a romance arc, after all, don't we? Especially the one who got all of her friends into this. I'm rooting for her to find love. A real underdog."

Oh god. He means Poppy.

"I have deposited gear, weapons, and what remained of the rations from the space station after I took over several hundred years ago somewhere near where you are sleeping. Retrieving them won't be easy, however, as I've also awoken the native fauna on this station's surface. I've also increased the signals to as much of space as I can, including the Draegon and Arco home planets. Those water dwellers are strange, but they do love a good mate hunt. It would be wrong of me to assist or hamper contestants, but I do love a good plot twist, so I absolutely will be. Whoever makes it to my control center alive wins. I'll be in touch!"

With that jaunty sign-off, the voice falls silent.

"What the hell is going on?" I ask. I'm so tense that if you slapped a blood pressure cuff on me, I'm pretty sure it would advise immediate hospitalization.

"I've heard about this. Everyone has. I always thought it was a story to scare children."

"Not everyone," I tell him, growing more anxious by the second.

His expression's worried, his gaze fixed on some point in the distance. "There was a space station—one of the first attempts at a cross-species colony. It was massive, the biggest ever built." A pause long enough that I can hear my blood pounding in my ears. "It was designed with a self-running, self-guided system, like nothing anyone had ever seen."

"Self-running?" I repeat, not getting it.

He says something in his language, and I blink, my translation software not doing anything to help.

"It didn't work." I tap my head. "No translation."

"Your species hasn't created this yet, then."

I'm not sure if that's a good thing or not, so I clamp my lips shut and wait.

"A false brain. It could think for itself, make decisions for the betterment of the entire population of the station." He shakes his head. "I do not know the term you would use."

"Artificial intelligence," I finally say, comprehension dawning.

A slow dawn, but a dawn nonetheless!

"More than that, but I suppose that is the general concept." He nods, a grim set to his face. Outside, a far-off clamor begins, so different than the silence I've grown accustomed to. I swallow, feeling the need to get up, to do something—and yet making myself move proves impossible.

I'm terrified.

"For a few years, the station seemed to be paradise. It worked well. The systems ran how they were supposed to. The inhabitants were healthy, they worked together."

I glance up at him, a muscle twitching in his jaw.

"Then it went dark. Completely dark. No contact was made, and when ships went out to investigate at the last known coordinates, there was nothing there. It was like it had vanished completely."

I shouldn't ask. I don't want to know. I have a feeling I already know.

"What happened?"

He tilts his head, then holds a hand out, gesturing at nothing and everything at once. "The system made choices for the people there. Now it's making choices for us."

"You think we're going to die?" It comes out in the smallest excuse for a whisper. Deep down, I know that's what happened to the people on that space station. They're dead. The AI killed them.

I wish I hadn't asked it.

"No." He sounds sure of himself. "I won't let that happen."

I want to believe him. I want to believe we're going to be okay, that my friends are going to be okay.

My legs are trembling.

"It said we were going to have to fight each other.

Those are my friends. I won't do it. I don't know how to fight, anyway."

His face gets hard, and he tucks his arm back around me.

Leaning into him is natural and soothing, and right now, I'll take any comfort I can get.

"You won't have to. We are going to figure this out."

No argument comes out, even though I want it to, because how can we figure this out? We're sitting ducks. Worse than sitting ducks because we have nowhere to fly.

I don't even have wings.

CHAPTER
TWENTY-FOUR

KA-REXSH

She's shaking. I have her as physically close to me as I can, and still, she's trembling all over, the smell of her fear clouding out her usual scent.

The need to take care of her is the most overwhelming instinctive drive I have ever experienced, on par with the need to breathe.

"Listen to me," I tell her, giving her a small shake.

Dazed, she stares up at me, her pupils huge with terror.

"We are going to do our best, do you understand? We are not going to give up, or do anything we cannot live with, because that is not who we are." It's not who I am.

There were many times, in the service of the king, that I chose to do better. To face punishment instead of mete it out.

"We will survive, and we will find a way through this."

Ellison continues to tremble. "I think we should have sex."

My jaw drops. Of all the things I expected her to say, that wasn't one of them.

I despise myself for how much I want to take her up on it.

"I am not going to mate with you under these circumstances, Ellison," I reply belatedly. "I won't coerce you, or let… this thing coerce you."

"It's not coercion." She shakes her head. "It's logic. I need to be able to function, and I can hardly think straight, thanks to the heat."

She has a point.

I hate it.

"No," I tell her in a clipped voice, ignoring the way my cock's painfully hard, skithing away in preparation for what she said she wants. "I won't let this take your choice from you."

"I am choosing to have sex with you to protect us both, and to take some pleasure before we have to…" she makes a noise of disgust, "survive out there. This might be the last chance we get."

"But you are not choosing to be mated to me," I say, the words soft.

Her head hangs, and then she tilts her face back up to me, a glint in her eyes. "No. Not yet. I am choosing to survive. You will have better odds if I'm not a feverish mess. We both need to be able to focus."

As if I would be able to focus with my heart walking around, in danger, beside me.

She's right, though. Once my mating poison has finished her heat, she'll be better.

Draegon females are stronger, faster after a sated heat. I won't tell her that, though, because I don't want to put any more pressure on her than there already is.

"It might hurt my ability to focus on anything but keeping you safe," I mutter.

"I don't see how that's a downside for me," she says.

I take a deep breath, trying to form some sort of coherent argument. "You don't want to be my mate."

"Not right now. Right now, I want to survive. After that? Who knows." Her gaze darts between my eyes, and I see nothing but truth reflected back at me.

What kind of mate would I be to deny her the increased safety of not being in heat?

"This isn't fair to you," I say softly, wishing I were stronger, wishing I could deny her and know it was the right thing to do.

"None of this is fair, not to any of us." Her tongue darts out as she licks her lips. "I want to live, Ka-Rexsh."

It's the first time she's tried to say my full name, and though I think the smaller version she uses is adorable, this sets me on fire, making my mind up for me.

"I'm sorry that I might not be able to give you what you want, though." Her brown eyes are huge in her face, and the fact she's apologized for that—for wanting to be alive, then for being worried about hurting me—it breaks something inside me wide open.

"I'm sorry that I don't have all the time in the world to make you love me. But I can give you this right now," I tell her.

She blinks up at me as I cup her face, and the runaway pace of her heart so loud I can hear it.

At first, I'm worried, worried I won't be enough for her, that I won't make it good for her in this limited time we have, but the minute I drag my mouth over hers, she grinds mindlessly against me, and all those worries disappear.

I lose all rational thought.

This is my female.

Maybe not forever, but for this moment, for the span of these breaths we share?

Ellison is mine.

CHAPTER
TWENTY-FIVE

ELLISON

I'm going to die if I don't get him inside me right away.

I mean, I might die anyway but what a way to go, huh?

My fingers rake at where the band of his pants meets his hips, beyond desperate to finally quell the need for him.

Not once in my life have I felt this insane need to have sex. It's been riding me from the moment he scraped the tip of his wing down my skin, yes, but I've mostly had it under control.

Now, though, in his arms, with the massive proof of his arousal right where I want it?

Yeah. What a way to go, ha!

He helps me pull his pants down because I'm too sweaty and shaky to do much. The logical part of my brain congratulates me on deciding to bang the alien because survival, am I right?

"I'm a survivor," I scream-sing at him, sweat dripping off the tip of my nose.

He doesn't seem to even notice the fact I'm as unhinged as a barn door after a cattle stampede, probably because I've wrapped my hand around his cock.

It's moving.

"What the hell is happening?" I ask. Not that it bothers me.

Nope. It looks like a one-way ticket on the G-spot pleasure cruise. I mean, yeah, it's daunting, but I'm past caring.

Scared and horny, that's me!

"It skiths for you," he says. "For your pleasure."

"Say less!" I cackle. This is gonna be aaaaaamazing!

"You want me to be silent?" he asks, cocking his head.

"Nah, Rex, I want you to talk me through it." I'm shucking clothes as fast as I can, and he's watching me with heavy-lidded eyes.

"Talk you through it?" he finally repeats.

"Yeah. Tell me how good it feels, what you like, what to do, you know, talk me through it."

I can't remember once in my life that I've told a man what to do in bed.

Apparently a mating heat danger bang really brings out the best in me.

"I need you." He nips at the soft spot underneath my ear, and I hiss out a breath. "You are beautiful. Perfect."

"Keep talking," I mutter. "Touch me."

"These are everything." He has my breasts in his hands, gaze reverent as he brushes his thumbs against my hard nipples.

That's all it takes for me to orgasm, but instead of taking the edge off, it just makes it worse.

Whining, I spread my legs, lining up his weird alien dick and then grinding down on it.

A strange choking noise surprises me until I realize it's coming from my mouth.

"Slowly, hyrulis. Slowly."

I don't know what that word means, but I whimper, doing as he instructs.

"So hot, so wet for me." His teeth graze my neck, and then he latches on a nipple.

I work him in deeper, inch by inch, sweat dripping between my shoulder blades. He feels… incredible.

Like a sex toy made just for me, but better—because he's real.

He's real, and he's looking at me like I'm better than chocolate ice cream.

"That is so good. You are everything," he says, hoarse. A smile curves my lips because knowing it's good for him makes it even better for me.

I slide him further in, and we both gasp, leaning our foreheads together, taking a moment to adjust to the sensation. It's more intimate, more special, than it has any right to be.

Then I feel it—the way his cock is moving, working inside me.

"Oh, oh," I moan, a second orgasm starting to build. I

rock against him, needy, and he does what I've asked. He talks me through it, his fingers gripping my hips so tight that it should hurt, but it just feels right.

"Tell me what you need," he demands. "Tell me what your body wants."

Wordless, unable to make any coherent noise, I grab his hand and put it between us, then cry out as he pulls it away from where I need it most.

"I don't want to hurt you, hyrulis," he says softly, before easily biting his talons off. He spits them to the floor, and it should be gross.

It's not.

It's hot.

So hot.

I move against him, chasing the release that's so close now.

"Show me where," he says, fingers dipping between my folds. Guiding him carefully, I put his newly shorn fingertips on my clit.

"Gentle," I hiss out, and it doesn't take him long to fall into a rhythm that matches what his cock is doing inside me.

It's too much.

It's not enough.

I lean forward, pressing my mouth against his, needing him everywhere I can get him. His tongue flicks against mine, and the orgasm plows through me like a freight train.

And a third one is coming right after it, like a little sex caboose.

"Chugga chugga choo choo," I moan.

"Choo choo?" Rex repeats, sounding dazed. "Is that what you call this?"

"It is now," I tell him, rolling us so he's on top. "I need more," I tell him. "I need it."

He grins down at me, a devilish light in those orange eyes, and I reach up, grabbing his horns on pure instinct.

"Hyrulis," he hisses.

Better than choo choo, I guess.

We ride that train (each other, ahem) until the feverish need to have sex has finally waned, and I'm sticky with our mutual release.

When we finally pull apart, my skin isn't nearly as hot.

Faint light shines through the window coverings. A new day is here, and everything has changed.

CHAPTER
TWENTY-SIX

KA-REXSH

My entire worldview has shifted.

I do not think I will ever be the same.

Now that I know what it can be like to be with a mate, I won't want anything else.

I don't know how I will let this human female go. But first, we have to get ourselves out of this nightmare in one piece.

Heaving a sigh, I glance at where my hyrulis has finished cleaning herself, dressing quickly.

"At least I have shoes now," she says, quirking a smile at me.

It's the first thing she's said since we did the life-changing mating, and it strikes me to the heart—not because it's some ground-breaking emotional confession, but for its companionable simplicity.

The kind of conversation that's easy and normal, in spite of the dire straits we now find ourselves in; the kind of remark one might make with their partner of years on end.

"That was fun, by the way." She holds her hand up, palm out to me, and I stare at it.

She expects something of me now, I'm sure of it, but I do not know this human hand tradition.

I hold my hand up like she is, level with my face, and watch her expectantly.

A smile brightens her face, and it's more beautiful than any sunrise on any world. Laughing, she presses her palm quickly to mine, her smile broader than ever.

"That's a high five," she explains, then turns to the bed we've only just left.

A high five. I file away this human post-coital ritual for later, pleased beyond belief that she's chosen to share it with me, even though she still does not want to be my mate.

This high five is a good sign.

Maybe I can coax enough high fives from her that she will want to high five with me and only me forever.

A sheet hangs half off the bed, the blanket at the corner, and Ellison tugs at the thinner of the two, popping it off completely.

"Do the same with the blanket," she tells me, pointing at the puddled fabric. "We can take shit with us. Make like a bag." She acts out slinging the sheet over her shoulder, and my eyes widen in understanding.

"This is very clever."

"It might be, it might not be," she says cryptically. "I would rather have things in case we need them than regret not grabbing anything."

"The station said we would have supplies."

"That we have to fight for." She makes a face. "I've never fought anyone."

"I will fight for us both," I tell her gravely. "It would be my honor."

"I can't say I've ever had anyone want to fight for me." Another bright smile, though this one is tainted by the slight trembling of her lower lip.

My mate is scared, and yet, she puts on a brave face.

I am scared, too, but her bravery makes mine grow.

"We should name it. The AI, I mean. It's weird to call it the station. It's not a station anymore, right? It's the AI. There's no one living here."

"It is dangerous to give things like that a name."

"Still. We're already in danger. Might as well make it easy to talk about."

I cock my head at her, tying the blanket corners into knots that will allow me to hook it over a shoulder. It will be in the way if I need to fly, but if it comes to that, then it will likely be too late to worry about the blanket, anyway.

"What do you think about the name Ken?" She narrows her eyes at nothing, still working on making neat knots of her own sheet. "Like the doll. Ken, no privates."

A laugh bursts out of her, quieted again just as quickly.

"The name means nothing to me," I tell her.

"Right. That's okay. We're calling it Ken."

"Ken No Privates," I dutifully repeat.

"He's just Ken," she says, choking on the words.

I pat her back. "Are you feeling alright?"

"Absolutely. Right. So what do you think we should try to take with us from here? Do you think we should look for the crew? Billie and Ayro? Do you think Ken is making them fight, too? This is so weird. Fuck!"

Brightness springs to her eyes, and pink suffuses her cheeks and a band across her nose. "I hate crying," she says, pinching the bridge of her nose with one hand, fanning her eyes with the other. "Distract me. Say something mean to me, make me mad."

"I would never." Outrage makes me nearly rip the blanket in two. "I would never say something mean to you."

"Not even if you were mad at me?" she asks, sniffling. A single tear tracks down her cheek.

"Not even then."

"I need a hug," she says, and before I can ask her to translate the word, she's flung herself into me, wrapping her arms around my waist, her wet face against my chest.

Oh. An embrace.

Slowly, I wrap my arms around her, too, enjoying the creature comfort of her touch.

Enjoying it, and loving that she's come to me for comfort.

Perhaps I stand a chance at being her chosen high five partner for life, after all.

CHAPTER TWENTY-SEVEN

ELLISON

We haven't made it far from the structure we spent the night in when Ken's weird voice booms all around us again.

"Welcome, contestants, to the first day of a *true* survival show." The AI pauses, for drama, I assume, after the absurd stress on the word true.

Like, we get it, Ken. You're trying to kill us. For funsies.

"I was lenient with all of you last night, while you grew accustomed to the new rules for *Mated and Afraid*. Some of you made very interesting choices. Don't worry, no one will be shown in coitus. Everything will be censored as deemed necessary per planet. So only the humans' planet, of course."

Oh shit. He's talking about us. Ken is talking about Rex and I having sex. Only being censored on Earth.

"Pervert," I mutter, kicking at a stone in my path. Rex stares at me curiously. Maybe pervert didn't translate.

"I heard that, Ellison," Ken says tartly. "Sticks and stones and words can hurt me."

I sigh. "That's not... you know what? Sure." There's no point in correcting the mixed metaphor.

For a split second, I wonder if Ken can be reasoned with. I wonder if, like Trent at work, he just requires a firm hand to lead him down the path of correct choices.

Of course, the moment I think it, Ken starts talking again, and the thought escapes me.

"Each of you are on a path I've created in the night. Each path will lead you through a set course of obstacles I tailored for each pair. If you go off the path, you will meet an untimely end. If you stay on the path, you have a chance at either meeting a more timely end or continuing on."

A more timely end? Is Ken still talking about dying? Or just ending... the game?

I don't know, but I'm going to assume the worst.

Normally, I wouldn't call myself a cynic, but right now? Assuming the worst is probably the best way to survive.

"The paths will ultimately lead to the control room, though you will be forced to meet along the way, and when you do, only one pair will be allowed to move on."

A pause.

I slide my hand into Rex's, grateful we decided to

have sex last night, beyond glad I'm no longer in heat, and grateful that I picked him as my partner. He makes me feel safe, and holding his hand reminds me that no matter how awful this is, I'm not alone.

We are in this together, for better or worse.

"No, Poppy, you can't just decide to quit."

Another pause, and my heart picks up at Poppy's name. She's trying to quit? She got us into this, and now she's going to quit?

"Because you signed a contract; you all signed a contract."

I inhale deeply. Poppy is a lawyer. "She knows the contract terms," I tell Rex. This is important. I wish I could hear whatever she's telling the AI to get it all in a huff.

"It does not specifically list fighting to the death as terms of the show—" Ken's voice cuts off, and Rex squeezes my hand.

"Of course you have a problem with the contract being replaced by my authority." Ken sounds sulky, if an AI could be sulky. "I want to produce a much more interesting show."

Hope springs in me, and I desperately wish I could hear Poppy right now.

She got us into this mess, and even though that pisses me off, I know with all my heart that if anyone can get us out of it, it's Poppy.

"Well, I didn't know that," the AI says, and there is definitely an annoyed, self-righteous tone now. "How could I have? I'm a more intelligent life form than any of you, but I'm not omniscient. We will discuss this without everyone listening." The voice snaps off, and the noisy sounds of the forest all around us restart.

"What is Ken No Privates talking about?" Rex asks me in a hushed tone.

The uncontrollable urge to giggle hits me, and I slap a hand over my mouth, knowing full well I better not laugh at this. Pissing off Ken, who holds our lives in the palm of his non-existent hand, is probably a real, real bad idea.

"Ah, I think my friend, Poppy, is trying to negotiate with Ken. She's a lawyer, and contract law is her specialty."

"Fascinating." Rex does, in fact, seem fascinated, and I shouldn't be annoyed at that. It's not like last night meant anything to me. Sure, it was the best sex of my entire life, but it was mostly a means of making sure I didn't die because the heat drove me out of my mind. "She is very intelligent, then, yes?"

"She's the reason we're all here," I snap at him. "This was her idea."

He stops, tilting his head at me, and when understanding lights his eyes, I scowl.

A wing brushes against my arm, and then he's holding me tight. "You're angry with me?"

"No." It comes out as glum and petulant as Ken just sounded. "We should probably keep moving."

"We should, but I want to know why you are upset."

"Poppy." The name drags out of me.

"It sounds like she is doing her best to help all of us.

Help me understand. You are still angry about being here?"

Frowning, I mutter the real reason under my breath, feeling stupid.

"Did you say you were jealous? Because I said her appeal to Ken No Privates based on the contract was intelligent?"

"He's just Ken," I say instead, refusing to look at him.

Embarrassed—I am so embarrassed.

His hand cups my chin, and I finally lift my eyes, gazing up at his handsome, strong face. "You are mine, no matter what you decide at the end of this. You have nothing to envy when it comes to any other female, ever. You can leave me, but you will take a piece of my heart with you." He thumps a fist on his chest.

"Ka-Rexsh," I murmur, just holding him for a long minute, trying to calm my pounding heart, trying to tell myself that we're going to be okay, that this isn't just the calm before the storm.

Finally, I sniffle again, brushing my hand against my cheek, and we start back down the trail, looking for the supply cache Ken said was somewhere on his chosen route.

It was the calm before the storm.

Literally.

Not five seconds after we started hiking down the path, all hell broke loose in the skies. Lightning forked down from thick storm clouds, followed by thunder so loud it made the ground shake.

Now, the rain's begun.

No gentle sprinkling, no warning whatsoever. Instead, an instant deluge, like a switch has been flipped.

Well, considering good ole Ken is involved, it very well could have been as simple as a switch being flipped.

My shoes, which I'd been so happy about, slosh with every step, taking on water like a leaky canoe my parents once rented on an ill-fated, last-minute camping trip. Camping was as close to a vacation as I ever got with my parents. Money, or lack thereof, stopped us from doing much more.

They always told me one day I'd appreciate it.

I don't think they meant I'd appreciate it because I was on an alien survival show where an AI was trying to torture us.

And yet!

Wet and miserable, I trudge along, barely able to see more than an arm's length in front of me. The gargantuan blue-tinged trees lining the path have all but disappeared in the onslaught, sheets of rain blocking them from view.

"Come here, hyrulis," Rex yells over the storm.

"I can't see you," I tell him. The next thing I know, I'm being tugged into his arms. It takes another moment for me to realize the rain has stopped.

No, not stopped. It's still pinging all around, but Rex's wings are blocking it out. He's made a shelter for me, and the heat from his body warms my wet skin almost instantly.

"Thank you." I nuzzle closer, trying to absorb all the heat I can.

Water sloshes in my shoes, even though I'm standing still.

"We need to keep moving," Rex says gravely.

Following his gaze, I look down.

The water wasn't sloshing in my shoes. It was racing over them, now lapping at the middle of my calves.

"Shit." It's flooding.

"No, just water," Rex says. "A shit flood would be much worse."

I don't know what to say to that, and I don't want to give the damned AI any ideas, so I keep my mouth shut.

"Are you a good swimmer?" he asks, face grim.

"I mean, I can swim. I have swum. Am I good at it?" I raise one shoulder. "I guess we're about to find out."

The water rises rapidly, now at my knees, tugging me off balance.

"Can you swim?" I ask him, and he nods, but he doesn't look confident. "Can you fly in this?" I'm yelling now, trying to be heard over the loud rush of the water and the thunder overhead.

"I am ashamed to admit that flying in this would be dangerous for me."

Something slides against my shin and I shriek, jumping up and nearly tackling poor Ka-Rexsh.

"What is it?" he asks, trying to see into the gloomy murk of the water.

"Probably just a fish. Or a log. Or something…" I leave the *or something* hanging in the air between us because I don't want to think about what it really felt like.

I shudder, though, and his arm tightens around my waist. "Ken said there would be supplies." It sounds pitiful, and I regret it the moment the words leave my mouth.

"We should drop what we are carrying."

I nod my agreement. The makeshift packs from sheets seemed like a really good idea at the time, but now they're more likely to pull us down into the water than be of any real use.

"With any luck, Ken was not lying." His voice is upbeat, but his face tells me he doesn't believe it.

It's looking increasingly like we're in serious trouble.

And it's being streamed.

For some reason, that motivates me more than anything else. The thought of all my coworkers seeing me drown on what is apparently not a moon and is, in fact, an abandoned alien space station pisses me off.

Like, really pisses me off, to a level of rage formerly reserved for the week before my period.

My eyes narrow.

Trent in particular—I can just imagine him watching. Gloating. Making a death pool with our other coworkers in the underwriting department. Getting paid out if I drown right now.

Buying another stupid stretchy polo shirt with the money.

"We're not DYING TODAY!" I bellow.

Fueled by pettiness and bad fashion, that's me.

I surge forward, refusing to let the possibility of

drowning enter my mind more than it already has. Or should I say flood my thoughts?

I let out a wild cackle, trying to tug Rex along beside me. It's a bit like trying to pull a pit bull along on a walk they don't want to partake in, though—until I realize the only reason it feels like we're moving in different directions is because the floodwaters are up to my thighs now.

"By the way," I shout at him, succeeding in getting a mouth full of rainwater. "I think whatever touched my leg was a giant snake."

A positively murderous light sparks in Rex's eyes, and I decide I'm very glad he's on my team.

Lightning slashes across the sky, so bright it sears my eyes—but not before I spy something bobbing in the distance.

Thunder booms, rattling the teeth in my mouth.

"A boat!" I point, the outline of the lightning still blinding me.

"I see it," Rex yells back, and he grips my upper arm tightly, keeping me upright as a wave of water buffets against us.

"Should we fly for it?"

I point up at the sky and mime flying as best I can when it becomes clear he can't hear me over the storm.

He nods despite the troubled look on his face.

Another bright spear of light forks across the clouds overhead, and he gathers me up in his arms, his huge thighs flexing as he vaults into the sky, wings beating furiously against the rain and wind.

Darkness tunnels in front of my eyes, and I suck in a huge breath until my lungs start to ache from holding it.

We're airborne. We're out of the flood.

I want to sob with relief, but I'll be damned if I'll give tight polo Trent the viewing pleasure of my own personal mental breakdown.

So I gulp another bit of air, lightning illuminating the boat bobbing on the rushing waters below us.

Rex's wings snap wide, and we glide down, down, towards where the boat rocks. The next thing I know, I'm yelping, thrown towards the boat—then I slam into it, rainwater in the hull splashing all around me.

Rex yells my name, and I cry out, reaching for him.

Then he's gone.

CHAPTER
TWENTY-EIGHT

KA-REXSH

At least my mate made it into the boat safely.

Water rushes up to my shoulders, but it's not the water I'm worried about at the moment. No, it's whatever's currently latched to my ankle and winding around my leg.

I kick at it, then take a deep breath and hope it isn't my last as water rushes around my head.

CHAPTER
TWENTY-NINE

ELLISON

"Oh, I think absolutely the fuck not," I rage.

My hands grip the edge of the boat, holding it so hard the metal side slices into the soft flesh of my palm. Blood drips down the edge of the boat and into the water.

"Perfect, I was really hoping to get tetanus out here," I yell. "Nothing like lockjaw to really complete this shitshow!"

Something slams against the boat, something finned and huge and terrifying, and all I can think is that if sharks can scent a drop of blood in an Olympic-sized pool, what are alien sharks' olfactory receptors like?

Much to think on.

Rex is gone. I can't see well enough to even know what happened, but I have a feeling the damned suspected snake that brushed up against me grabbed him. Either that, or something else did.

There's no way Mr. Let's Mate Forever just threw me into the boat then dove into the floodwaters on his own.

No. Way.

Gritting my teeth, I turn back to the boat, almost certain that good old sadistic Ken No Privates gave me a way of getting my man back.

Partner. Alien. Man.

Whatever.

Ignoring the sting of the new cuts on my palms and the creeping, horrifying feeling that there is something huge under the boat, I balance as well as I can. I squint through the murky rain, trying to find the so-called supplies Ken promised.

"I get that you wanted to put on a good show, but this is fucked up," I yell.

Maybe it's my imagination, or wishful thinking, but the rain does seem to let up, just a little. Huh.

Wiping the water from my eyes, I finally spot what I'm looking for—hopefully. Only one way to find out. The boat's a weird cross between a pontoon and a canoe, metal benches spanning the width, and underneath one, the prize I was looking for: a metal tacklebox, like the one my dad used to keep his sparkly fishing lures in.

"We're gonna need a bigger boat," I say, laughing maniacally, lightning punctuating the remark.

"Hope you had a close-up going for that line," I yell at Ken, who is no doubt listening in, the creep. "Are you not entertained?"

Russell Crowe would be proud. I have no idea who wrote *Jaws*, but I doubt they would mind my little stress-fueled allusion. Of course, Russell Crowe's character died in the end of *Gladiator* and most of the *Jaws* cast did, too.

A splash catches my attention, and Rex's green head surfaces in the foaming water long enough for him to take a deep breath.

He's still alive, and I'm gonna do my best to keep him that way.

The latches on the tacklebox are slippery from the rain, which has subsided a little further, but I manage to pry them open and tug the whole heavy box into the standing water at the bottom of the weird boat.

I haven't fallen overboard yet, but I need to hurry if I have a shark's chance in a Spielberg movie of saving my Draegon alien.

I file away the thought of him being mine to look at later, rummaging through the huge box. There's foil-wrapped packages that look suspiciously like MREs, and I ignore them, opening up the next layer as fast as I can.

My hands are shaking from adrenaline and the cold, and then I see it.

A big old knife. I have no idea what kind of knife it is, true, because the knives I've handled could all easily be designated into three categories: butter, steak, and the big kitchen one I have to be careful using so I don't slice my finger off.

This knife'll do, pig.

A plan forms, a stupid, dangerous plan, but it's better than nothing.

"Snake," I crow. "It's what's for dinner."

Lightning flashes, the reflection sparkling off the blade and very nearly blinding me. Ken must have a flair for dramatic cinematography. Good for him, we all need hobbies.

I'm already bleeding, so that part of my hare-brained plan is taken care of, at least, until I spot the plastic package labeled "bait" in screaming red letters.

If I know my reality TV, and I sure as shit do, I am supposed to use this.

There's no way I'm not supposed to use this.

Plus, it will likely be doubly potent with my blood. I mean, maybe. I don't know much about fishing and hunting or killing giant alien snakes, but adrenaline has only steered me wrong ninety percent of the time.

I kneel in the bottom of the boat, not willing to lose my balance and fall overboard at the wrong time.

Yes, must fall overboard at the RIGHT time for this plan to work.

It sure as shit better work because I am not doing this reality thing alone. Rex isn't getting out of this that easy. Nope, no way, no how.

The cut on my hand isn't bleeding as fast and furious as it was, and I decide right here and now that if I'm going to do this, I'm going to make sure I do it right.

First things first, though.

I pull off my shoes, tying them together and looping them around one of the support struts anchoring a bench to the boat. I'll be faster in the water with my shoes off.

An unhinged laugh comes out of me, because it's either that or cry.

"Go, hyrulis, Ellison, save yourself." Rex's voice is closer to the boat now, the current from the floodwaters pushing him downstream.

"Fat fucking chance," I yell back.

Lightning flashes long enough to illuminate his gorgeous face, a jagged cut running down his cheek and dripping blood.

Yeah, that's not gonna work for me.

I need to make a bigger entrance. I need to outshine my Draegon.

"My time to shine, attention hog," I scream at Rex.

He's too busy trying to pull the alien snake off him to clock that bit of adrenaline-fueled weirdness.

A scaled tail slaps the water, the tip of it curling around his horn and jerking his head back under.

Thunder sounds, and I've already waited too long. I have a sneaking suspicion the longer Rex fights the thing, the worse the odds will be for my partner.

I tear open the packet labeled "bait," and a foul stench immediately makes me gag.

Note to self: do not inhale freshly opened bait pouches.

It's too late, though, and I throw up over the side of the boat.

More chum. Yum yum.

Still gagging, I dump the disgusting contents of the pouch into the water. The knife floats next to me, and I pick it up, biting my lip.

"Ah, fuck it," I say, then slice the wound from the edge of the boat deeper, until blood runs thick into the water.

It hits me at the same time as the huge thing under the water slams into the boat—this probably wasn't my best or brightest idea.

We're not gonna survive this.

CHAPTER
THIRTY

KA-REXSH

The creature is a horrifying mix of razor-sharp teeth, stacked twenty rows deep, and thick, muscled coils. Fins fan out behind a set of jagged gills, too close to the monstrous mouth for me to attempt to strike it there.

I don't have my talons on one hand—I broke them off to better please Ellison, and I can't make myself regret that.

At least I will have died having brought her pleasure.

The creature tightens around my chest, and I cry out as one of the bones in my left wing snaps under the pressure. My mouth clamps shut, and I rake my talons over the beast's hide, the little good that it does.

I have Ellison.

I have a reason to live.

I could have a future.

I want her in it.

The thoughts tangle, growing as murky as the water all around us.

It's so silent in the water, so quiet.

I surface again, gasping for air, air that's hard to come by with the creature squeezing the life from me.

A flash of light.

Ellison hangs over the boat, holding her palm out, a stream of crimson coloring the water below.

The serpent's coils loosen.

"No." The word comes out weak, weaker than I could have imagined. She's trying to get it to pick her instead as a meal, trying to divide its attention between us.

I take a deeper breath, my chest finally able to more fully expand. Until a sharp pain seizes me up.

Shallow breathing instead, then.

I kick my legs as the beast loosens its coils from around me, the massive tail knocking me sideways as I try to make my way towards Ellison and the boat.

"It's coming for you," I shout at her.

"I'm ready, Rex." She holds up a knife that's the length of her forearm. "I have a plan."

Its hide is impenetrable. My talons proved that very quickly.

"Swim for the boat," she screams. "Hurry."

I don't waste time thinking about it. I swim, and I hope to whatever god might be watching that the eldritch screaming isn't hers.

My wing drags behind me in the water, pain shooting from the tips all the way to my shoulder blades. Flight isn't an option now, and it won't be later, not until I heal.

If I get the chance to heal.

Lightning flashes again, dazzling in the dark of the storm, though it is no longer raining as hard.

What I see sends a jolt of fear all the way down to my toes.

The many-toothed serpent is wrapped around something out of a nightmare. A huge monster, some horrible combination of tentacles and razor-sharp teeth. Jet-black eyes pay me no heed as I take in the battle in front of me. The newcomer gnaws on the hide of the serpent, who screams again, lashing in the water.

Ellison is still in the boat, screaming for me to swim.

I do as she asks.

Finally, I'm at the boat, and she's doing her best to pull me in. My wing is dead weight behind me.

I don't care. She is alive. I am alive.

We're together.

"There's a motor," she yells at me. "I think I can drive it."

With that, she leaves me sitting in several inches of water, stunned and hurt, but alive. Blood seeps from a dozen jagged wounds, and I can't move my wing or breathe too deeply, but I'm alive.

"You saved me," I croak out. "How did you know that thing would..." I cut my gaze to where the alien beasts are still fighting.

"I gambled," she says gaily, then laughs hysterically.

A mechanical rumble starts, and I hold onto a bench in front of me with one hand as Ellison laughs and laughs, the sound eventually drowned out by the boat's engine as she cuts through the water.

CHAPTER
THIRTY-ONE

ELLISON

By the time the rain stops, I'm shaking all over. My teeth are chattering.

Rex is asleep, one cheek against the bench, his body folded into itself.

The cut on my hand stopped bleeding. Maybe an hour ago, maybe less, maybe more. It's impossible to tell how much time has passed.

My stomach grumbles, and I shade my eyes against the sun now peeking out from the clouds.

I cut the engine, afraid that if I keep driving while I'm this tired we'll end up rammed into a tree or worse. Who knows what Ken is capable of?

We don't have Barbie here to tell us.

Tears threaten, and even though having a nice cry would be totally warranted right now, I know it will both give me a migraine and probably make my work enemies happy.

"Fuck you, frenemies," I mutter. "May this show find you distinctly unwell."

Ah yes, pettiness, my fine feathered friend. I glance around and try to get a grip.

"We made it," I say out loud, sinking to one of the benches. We made it past the first AI challenge.

And damn, did it suck.

I stretch my leg out, my feet wet and waterlogged from standing so long, and my toes brush up against the tacklebox.

Food.

I need calories, and I need rest, and I need to make a new plan.

Of its own accord, my hand reaches up and pats me on the back.

"Good job on the last plan, me," I say out loud.

Rex stirs but keeps sleeping.

The sight of him, alive, asleep, makes me smile, warmth from it helping my teeth finally stop chattering.

I lower my voice. "Okay. Next plan: Tacklebox supply catalog. Eat food, take care of Rex, take care of my hand. Dry out shoes." I glance at where they're hanging in the water, the knot in the laces still holding up.

Thunder rumbles overhead, but it sounds so quiet and far-off now that I don't even bother looking up.

The tacklebox is what I need to focus on.

I hadn't bothered refastening the latches, so when I open it up again, there's a fair amount of water in the first tray holding what I sure as shit hope are rations. The first silver foil pack glints in the watery sunlight, and I eye it with increasing suspicion. I don't know what's written on it, and my translator isn't providing any sort of feedback on what could be in the packets.

I decide to ignore my hunger for now.

Definitely not worth trying to eat something that might poison me.

Water droplets spray as I pull up the first level, revealing the second tray where I'd found my knife. The knife I forgot about in my rush to get away from the weird-ass monster cage fight. A glance tells me it's fine, on the bench directly in front of the motor-thing I'd somehow managed to get working and steered all the way to where we are now.

I mentally add "figure out where we are" to the to-do list.

The tray holds a few smaller knives, and I eye them suspiciously without one clue as to what they could be for. I have my big bad knife, and I'm happy enough with him that I don't feel like even looking at these smaller ones.

They creep me out a little.

Sighing, I lift the third tray, and I can't contain my cry of joy at what I find inside it. Of all the things, this is something I definitely know how to use.

"A comms pad," I say reverently, pulling out the brand-new piece of tech and hugging it to my chest like it's an old friend. Hopefully Big Bad Knife doesn't get jealous.

Finally, I stop hugging it and stare down at it. It's not far off from the tablet I used on Earth, and this model is one I'd been drooling over for a few months. It takes me a couple seconds to turn it on and program it to my biometrics, and I squeal in renewed delight as the contacts app pops up, revealing the names I wanted to see most in the world.

"Thank you, Ken," I say reverently.

Poppy. Lily. Lucy. Selene.

God, I hope this means they're still alive. Did they go through the same shit we just did? I have no idea.

Now I can find out, though.

My hands are still trembling badly enough that it takes me much longer than it should to set up a group chat. Water drips on the screen and I wipe it away, thinking it's raining again, before I realize I'm crying.

> Ellison: Are you all okay? Did you find your comms tablets?

I realize as soon as I've sent it that the second question is super redundant, seeing as how they won't be able to message back unless they've located a tablet of their own.

I hope my friends are okay.

The thought turns my overwhelming fear for them into something else, something I didn't really expect after the adrenaline rush of saving Rex and getting us safe.

Rage. Pure, unadulterated rage. Not at Poppy, though blaming her would be easy enough, or at myself, because I certainly did sign up for the damned show—but at the

AI who took us from fun reality premise to actual life-or-death danger.

I'm gripping the screen so tightly that the cut on my palm opens back up, blood dripping down my thumb and over my wrist.

> Selene: we're alive
>
> Lucy: same, barely

Poppy sends something too, but the message is blacked out as though it's been censored.

Nothing from Lily.

I inhale, and it's a shaky sob.

> Ellison: Anything from Lily?
>
> Poppy: Not yet
>
> Ellison: God, I hope she's okay. Are any of us... okay though, really?
>
> Selene: This place is a trip, but better than some situations I've found myself in
>
> Selene: Trust me, you're all better off here, anyway

Ew. That does not sound good. My finger hovers over the comms tablet and I chew my lip. How do you even respond to that?

> Poppy: fuoking AI

I suppose you could completely change the conversation, instead of responding, à la Poppy.

> Poppy: Bad enough AI is ruining our water supply on Earth and churning out ugly art, but now one is actively trying to kill us? I don't love it
>
> Ellison: his name is Ken

I'm not sure why it's important to insist on that, but it is to me.

> Selene: At least we weren't abducted by mercenaries this time
>
> Lucy: You want to talk about it?

Yeah, that's pure Lu. She's never met a stranger, I swear.

The boat rocks gently as Rex carefully moves to sit next to me, pulling me into his lap and using one wing as a sunshield.

"Thank you," I say softly. He's okay. We're okay.

> Selene: No

Right. That solves that. For now.

> Poppy: Ken agreed to abide by the contracts we signed. We can't opt out now, but if we are critically injured or ill Ken will do his best to assist

> Poppy: I am so sorry. I cannot begin to make this right

I take a deep breath because I know Poppy, and I know she's beating herself up for this.

> Ellison: We're going to make it out of this

> Poppy: In good news, he has also agreed to not kill any of us off, so when we complete his new ideas for the show, we all get to go to Sueva.

I'm not sure how legally binding Ken's word is, but I look up at the clouds still blotting out most of the sun overhead anyway. "Thank you, Ken."

"Where did you find the tablet?" Rex asks. I glance up at him, warmth spreading through me at the sight of him, whole, talking, right here next to me.

"I'm so glad you're okay," I say, and I'm sobbing again. So much for not having a migraine. "I was so scared."

"You took a very big risk, a risk you shouldn't have," he says, and there's a note of censure in his voice. I open my mouth to argue, but he presses his against mine, and whatever I was going to say dies on my lips as he kisses me.

"But you saved my life. You are incredible, hyrulis."

"I don't know what that means," I whisper. My hand finds his cheek, the other still clutching the tablet, and I soak him in as he stares down at me.

"It translates to…" He pauses, and my fingers wander up to his temple, then to the gentle striations of his horn. "Queen of my heart. Treasure of my life." His orange eyes meet mine, and my heart skips a beat.

"No one's ever called me anything like that."

"You should know how precious you are."

The comms tablet dings, and we both look back at it.

> Lily: this whole place is fucking fucked
>
> Lily: I'm so glad you're all alive. And I guess we're all staying alive? Shit. Shit!
>
> Lily: Good job working that out, Pops
>
> Lily: we're alive too. I think my ankle is sprained, but Zan is making me a brace right now
>
> Lily: I would say let's try to meet up, but I think the AI is going to actively keep us from that
>
> Poppy: You are correct. Ken wants us separated. I tried to change that, but there was nothing to work with in the contract when it came to that.
>
> Lucy: I gotta go
>
> Selene: Same. Be safe
>
> > Ellison: Let's check in each morning and night, okay? I will feel better if I know you're all okay.
>
> Poppy: we can't discuss strategy, FYI

Poppy: That's why that one message was censored

Poppy: We should all get back to work though. I get the feeling Ken doesn't like down time

I like their responses, sending my own goodbyes.

"I think there's food in the tacklebox, but I'm not sure," I tell him. I'm embarrassed to sniffle again, overcome with the rush of emotions from finding out my friends are okay. We're okay, and this little game is going to be a shit ton more dangerous than we bargained for, but at least the imminent threat of death is off the table.

"You are a worthy partner. A worthy mate. I only hope I can be worthy of someone like you."

My jaw drops, but he's already carefully making his way to the tacklebox, not waiting for me to say anything in return.

He truly expects nothing from me when it comes to returning his feelings, especially now that I'm not in heat.

The surprising thing is, I'm finding it harder and harder to not return them.

Ka-Rexsh is a good partner. I know, deep inside, he would be a good mate, too.

CHAPTER
THIRTY-TWO

KA-REXSH

The first tray of the box is full of extremely rare, extremely expensive medication designed to help repair the integumentary and skeletal systems on a cellular level. They aren't Draegon-made, but a product of Arco research, which Ellison apparently doesn't have programmed into her translator.

As soon as I explain to her what it does, I immediately tear open a packet and drink the gel-like substance within.

It's going to hurt, but I'd rather heal fast and painfully than not be able to fly or protect my mate.

The second tray is full of carrier knives, designed to deliver potent poisons.

The third tray held the comms tablet Ellison's hugging to her chest, along with a charging device.

The bottom and largest section of the box contains an ancient-looking water purifier, a fire starter, a length of rope, and a length of thick-gauged wire.

"That looks like the stuff they'd give competitors on one of the off-grid shows," Ellison says. "I don't know how we're supposed to use any of it with all this water."

I don't mention that I have other ways of starting a fire because this very well may be a wiser way to keep my woman warm and fed than to put all my cards on the table in front of an entity as unpredictable as Ken.

"I am sure we will find out, hyrulis," I tell her. The name is perfect for her, and I don't think I could stop using it even if she hated it. "Are you hurt?" I hold out a packet of the gel to her, but she shakes her head.

"Not even for the cut on your hand?" It was bleeding freely enough to have left a stain on the steering mechanism for the boat's motor.

"It's not that bad. I'd rather save it in case something worse happens," she says slowly.

"Show me," I demand.

Frowning, she holds her hand out to me, slowly uncurling her fingers. A gash runs across her palm, but she's right—it's not deep, and it's not bleeding anymore.

I hate it all the same.

I hate that she mutilated herself to save me.

"I want you to take the medicine anyway." I clear my throat, trying to cut the growl out of my voice. "To prevent infection."

"That's not a bad idea. But what if something worse happens? Like a compound fracture?"

My translator provides an image of a bone jutting through her delicate skin, and I snarl in response.

Ellison blinks.

"Congratulations, players," Ken's voice interrupts the apology I was about to form. "You have each conquered the first *real* challenge of *Mated and Afraid*, though your completion didn't come without a cost, did it? Looking at you, Selene!"

"Oh no," Ellison says on an exhalation. "Poor Selene. I hope she's okay."

I rip open the packet of medicine for Ellison, and she takes it absently, still listening to the AI she's named Ken.

"Prince Pol certainly has his hands full with that one, doesn't he, folks? All of you have found your comms tablets, and somehow even the evolutionarily stunted humans have figured out how to work them. Truly a surprise around every corner here on *Mated and Afraid*—too stupid to protect their planet from themselves, but smart enough to work technology. A conundrum of the worst sort."

I arch an eyebrow at Ellison, curious if what it says is true. Did they destroy their planet?

She gives me a grim nod in response, and I frown. I knew the humans had barbaric traditions, but I did not know they were actively killing their planet.

How bizarre.

"You will have tonight to recover from today's fun, so I suggest you all find a secure location to sleep, eat, and rest up for tomorrow's adventure. Those of you who are still in heat, you may want to reconsider holding out.

Those of you who have mated, you will receive a bonus prize when you settle in your campsite. Congratulations again, and good luck!"

With that, the voice fades away, replaced by the water lapping at the metal sides of the boat.

"It's lower now," I observe. The trees, which were nearly completely submerged, now poke from the flood like strange markers on our watery road.

"Much lower," she agrees. "Do you think Selene is okay? And her Draegon... what's his name... Pol is a prince?"

"It is strange that he is here." It's not really an answer and she tilts her head, waiting for one.

"Yes. He is a prince, one of the heirs. He left our home world long ago." I fall silent. Pol's story is not mine to tell.

That, and refusing to speak ill of the mad king is an old habit learned through pain.

It won't be easy to break, I fear, not even on Sueva.

"If anyone can take care of the human woman, it is Pol," I tell her, and I mean it. "He was a mercenary, an assassin. He is formidable, and if she chose him as her mate, then he will not rest until she is safe and healthy."

"He doesn't sound that different from you." Ellison's voice is soft.

I scoff. "He is a prince. Of royal blood. He was raised with a sword in his hand and the constant threat of violence from the rest of his family. I am glad we will not have to fight him."

"You could beat him."

A laugh trickles out of me at that, but it's not mean. "That is kind of you."

There's a stubborn set to her jaw, and fire in her eyes. "I mean it, Rex. You went after that awful snake. You fought it even though it..." She motions to my wing. "It hurt you, and you didn't give up."

"I did not have many options but to fight the serpent," I tell her wryly. "You are the one that saved me."

"You would have done the same for me."

I nod. "I would have. I would have done the same for you without a second thought."

The boat rocks slightly as she sits next to me.

I don't move, afraid to ask for too much, to overwhelm her, when I can sense her emotions are unstable.

"The medicine helped," she says.

Her cheek lands on my shoulder, and I can't resist touching her again. My arm wraps around her shoulders, pulling her close to me.

"I am glad, hyrulis," I murmur.

Her breath is warm, and it gradually evens out as she relaxes against me.

"I'm glad you're my partner for this," she says, glancing up at me. A lock of her damp red-brown hair falls into her face, and I tuck it behind her ear.

"I am pleased to hear you say that," I tell her. I am, too, the comment leaving me warm all over, distracting me from the pain of the medicine rebuilding my wing and my ribs.

We stay like that for a long while, drifting among the flooded alien pines.

CHAPTER THIRTY-THREE

ELLISON

The sky is a freakishly bright purple, the sun setting impossibly fast.

It gets colder the moment it starts descending behind the treetops, much higher now that the water has completely disappeared.

I fell asleep against Ka-Rexsh, and only woke up when the boat bumped against the ground.

It wasn't a solid sleep, and I'm still exhausted from everything today, so the thought of getting a full night's sleep on solid ground without worrying about being attacked by something awful the AI throws at us sounds phenomenal to me.

"It makes me uncomfortable," I say out loud.

"What does?"

"The path. It's unnatural."

He grunts, nodding and squeezing my hand. "Ken is leading us somewhere." Ka-Rexsh's wing looks like it must be getting better because he's holding it up, though it's still at an awkward angle.

"Are you in pain?" I ask him.

"Yes," he says, and it's matter-of-fact. He's not complaining, not whining, not throwing a fit about it. He's in pain, and he's handling it.

"You're very strong," I tell him.

He shoots me an amused look.

"In the physical sense, obviously," I rush on. "But mentally, too. You haven't complained about your wing, or any of those cuts from that awful snake, and you're taking care of me."

I run out of words, wrinkling my nose in irritation at myself.

How embarrassing can I be?

"Taking care of you is an honor, Ellison. The pain in my wing isn't worth wasting more energy complaining about, especially when I could spend the time hearing your voice instead of my own. I will not lie, though, I am pleased that we are on the way to a safe place to sleep for the night, and I am pleased that your friend Poppy was able to reason with Ken." He shakes his head, frowning. "It's odd. All of this."

"I worry about Billie and Ayro and the rest of the crew."

"You have a kind heart," he tells me, squeezing my hand again.

"No one has ever accused me of that," I say with a laugh.

He gives me a quizzical look, and I assume that particular colloquialism didn't translate quite right.

The light's fading. "We should walk faster. I can't see in the dark."

"I can," he says easily. "I think the campsite is directly ahead."

He puts an arm around my waist, leading me to the site. While I can't see the campsite, I don't really need his help walking, but it's nice to be helped.

It's nice to be cared for.

I'm not sure I remember the last time I let someone take care of me.

I'm not sure I remember if anyone ever wanted to.

A branch snaps in the distance, and if it startles Ka-Rexsh, he doesn't show it. Our steps are loud, too, but unlike the previous nights here, there are a multitude of forest noises now. Soft bird calls—at least, I hope they're birds—and rustling leaves, the susurrus of insects.

"How did they live through the flood?" I ask out loud, surprising myself.

"I don't know," Rex answers grimly. "I have a feeling that Ken is populating the surface of this place as he sees fit."

"What do you think happened here?"

It's a dangerous question to ask, considering Ken is likely listening in, and setting him off would be a definite hazard to our health.

"I don't know." He shakes his head, giving me a meaningful look.

It's funny how we've only been together a couple of days because I know exactly what he's thinking—Rex also thinks pissing off Ken is a bad idea, and the topic of whatever happened to all the people who once lived here is absolutely a no-go topic of conversation.

Still. I can't help wondering.

"How many?" I ask, and he shakes his head again.

I don't blame him. "Curiosity killed the cat," I say out loud.

"You brought a cat?" he replies, thoroughly flummoxed.

A laugh bursts out of me, and I'm grinning at him as we step into a clearing. Rex stops, and I look around warily, then realize this is a pretty good approximation of a campsite on Earth. A pile of rocks circles a round pit, and a couple of sleeping bags are rolled up next to it.

It's barebones, but it's dry, and at this rate, that's a shit ton more than I expected.

Ka-Rexsh is already kneeling by the firepit, and I'm pleasantly surprised to see there's even wood in it already. The tacklebox sits next to him, and he digs through it and quickly finds the fire starter. With an expert flick of his fingers, the fire starter sparks, and before I can so much as blink, the kindling ignites.

"That was impressive," I say, hugging my arms against my chest to ward off the cold.

He grins at me, the firelight gleaming off his sharp canines. "You are easy to impress, then."

"Maybe I am." I laugh, shrugging slightly. "Do we need more wood?"

"I'm not sure we want to burn any of these trees," he says, frowning at them. "This type of tree, on my planet, is full of sap. It's not good to burn. Beside, I don't want you to be alone here while I search for wood."

"I could help you look." I'm slightly miffed that he would leave me here.

"You cannot see in the dark."

"That is a problem. You're not wrong," I admit, laughing at myself. "Will you hand me the comms tablet, please? I'm going to check in with the other women."

He nods and hands it to me wordlessly, and the tablet screen shines bright enough that I have to back out and adjust the settings so it doesn't blind me in the darkness.

I scooch back to the main screen, fingertip hovering over the comms app, when I see something that makes me squeal in utter delight.

Which, of course, freaks poor Rex out completely.

"What is wrong, hyrulis?" he asks, head swiveling so fast as he tries to figure out where the danger is coming from that I can't help laughing again.

"Nothing is wrong, I'm sorry I scared you. Look." I hold up the comms tablet, pointing to the app I just noticed. "This is my favorite reading app—it's for fanfiction. I mean, I have no idea how this could possibly work here, but if it does? I'm going to be so happy." I hug the tablet to my chest, absurdly pleased.

"Fanfiction?" he asks. "This word does not translate."

"Oh." My nose wrinkles, and I tilt my head. How the

heck am I supposed to explain that I've been reading fan stories about humans being abducted by sexy aliens since the Roth invaded and we realized aliens were real? Every new tidbit of information we learn about the aliens led to new stories being written at such a rapid-fire, frenzied pace that it provided me with hours of entertainment. And then there are the other fanfics, too, all about popular series or books that people wanted to change to make the characters do something different, or the fics about celebrities, or the alternate universe fics—but I never really read any of those.

Nope. I'm an alien fanfic girlie through and through.

"It's stories," I say in a hoarse voice that sounds guilty even to my ears. "I mean, it's more than that, but it's just made-up stories, basically."

How the heck do I explain the gold that is fanfic to an alien?

"You screamed in excitement."

"They're the best stories," I gush, plopping on the ground and opening up the app. I have my username and password memorized, of course, and the app lets me log in with no issues. "It's all these writers who love these really specific ideas or certain characters and they just write them with wild abandon. They write for themselves, and to have a good time, and you can tell. It's just fun."

He sits next to me, the fire dancing merrily as more of the logs in the pit catch. "What's your favorite?"

I squirm, uncomfortable. "You don't want to know that."

Rex gives me a long, searching look. "Why would I ask you that if I didn't want to know?"

"You can't make fun of me," I tell him, drawing a circle in the dirt with the toe of my shoe. "I should probably take these off so they can finish drying."

Call me the master of the subject change.

"I won't make fun of you." He scoots down, unlacing my boots and pulling them off, setting them next to the fire. The socks follow, and I cringe at the sight of my water-logged skin. I have blisters. My blisters have blisters. "Hyrulis. Why didn't you tell me your feet pained you?"

"We're both hurting. The blisters will heal."

"You're taking another gel pack."

"We should save them—"

"No. You risk infection. We are not saving them when you need them now."

Grumbling, I take the foil pack from his hand and slurp down the bitter stuff, because he's not wrong.

I just sincerely hope we don't wish we'd saved them.

"We have one left," he says, closing the tacklebox. "Now tell me about your favorites. I will not make fun of you, I swear." He raises three fingers and holds them sideways.

"Three?" I cock my head at him.

"It's a symbol of honor with my people. Stop changing the subject."

"Fine," I exhale. "My favorite are the alienabductionfanfics." The words bleed together as I say it as fast as I can.

He leans forward, his dark hair falling around his face. "What? I did not understand."

"Alienabductionfanfics." It comes out even faster.

"It is not translating." He points to his ear. "You might have to explain it differently."

I'm saved from that particular mortification by swirling, glowing dust motes. They rotate like a tornado, casting a green light as they fuse together, moving faster and faster.

"What fresh hell is this?" I screech and hop into Rex's lap, which is probably stupid, because now his hands are full of me instead of weapons.

The light solidifies, making a shape that's vaguely hominid.

"Good evening, contestants. I'm here to present you with a special luxury reward challenge for your evening." The face in the light is spooky, a cross between a person and a freaky noseless mask.

That voice, though. I recognize it.

"Ken?" I ask, my voice ratcheting up a few octaves.

"The one and only," he says cheerily.

"Ken No Privates?" Rex stands up, still holding me as he circles around the figure of light.

"Just Ken," he tells Rex, sounding annoyed.

"Are you a hologram?" I ask, fascinated.

"He's Just Ken No Privates," Rex tells me.

Ken ignores that. I bite my cheeks to keep from laughing out loud.

That's probably not the ideal response with him standing right there. Er. Projected right there.

Whatever.

"Contestants, tonight your luxury reward challenge is a puzzle. If you finish the puzzle within the time constraints, you receive both a meal and a luxury shelter for the night."

"And if we don't finish it in time?" I ask.

Just Ken No Privates ignores that, too.

A grinding sound begins near the fire, and Rex takes several big steps back as the ground parts, a table of rock rising out of nothing. Pain streaks across my palm, and I loosen my too-tight hold on the tablet when I realize I have the darn thing in a total death grip.

"You have one hour to complete the puzzle. Good luck."

"Wait, you said we'd get a reward for, er, consummating—" the word sticks in my throat, but I push it out anyway, "the mate bond."

"Your reward is a slightly easier puzzle, in line with your lack of mental acuity."

I wince. "Ouch."

With that, the green hologram fizzles out, leaving us alone.

Though we're not, not really. Ken is watching. Good ole AI Big Brother. Oh, and whoever else is watching the show, too. We are far from alone, and I should remember that. I swallow hard, my jaw tight.

A chime comes from the table, and Rex slowly puts me back on my feet. He takes my hand, then presses a kiss against my knuckles, almost mindlessly, as we both approach the new stone dais.

The sweet gesture eases my nerves slightly, and I feel better.

Until I see the puzzle.

There's no way we're getting that luxury reward.

CHAPTER
THIRTY-FOUR

KA-REXSH

Ellison is mumbling about poop and building blocks under her breath, according to the words my translator is supplying.

"Shit... bricks?" I repeat, thoroughly amused. Ellison is more than I bargained for—pretty, smart, brave, and endlessly entertaining, especially when she's grumpy like right now.

"Exactly." She nods furiously. "Shit bricks."

"I do not think bricks made of shit would help us right now," I tell her delicately, trying not to laugh at her.

She rakes a hand through her hair, which make it even more tangled and poufy than it was. Adorable.

"I just, I thought it was going to be a puzzle, you know? Like, a jigsaw puzzle. We could have a cozy night, put together the jigsaw puzzle, make a picture, and go to sleep." She waves a hand at the puzzle in front of us, irritated. "This isn't a jigsaw puzzle."

"A jigsaw puzzle? You humans make puzzles out of construction equipment? Do you actually use said shit bricks?"

She makes an indistinct noise of frustration, her brow wrinkled, then she stares at me a moment longer and lets out a long laugh. "No. No—I don't know why it's called that. It's just a picture cut up into little pieces and then you put them together."

"Why would you cut up art?"

Her lips purse. "The whole thing is just for fun." Brown eyes narrow. "Why aren't you worried about this puzzle?"

"Probably because I am not being squeezed to death by a serpent while my mate bleeds into the water and I can't get to her."

"Ah." She nods. "That does sound slightly more stressful."

The way Ellison says it is so dry that I can't help a laugh of my own.

We both grin at each other across the puzzle table, and then she taps the little screen displaying a ticking clock.

"We better get to work."

I nod, turning as much of my full attention to the puzzle on the table as I can. There are two screens, one with the clock, and the other displaying what I can only assume is the puzzle we're supposed to solve. It's a diagram of sorts, a series of rectangles, each with an opening.

"It says: draw a continuous line through each of the doors without the line ever intersecting or using any door more than once." Ellison drags her finger through a series of the doors, and a trail of color follows the motion.

Soon, though, she's stuck, and the screen flashes red before the line erases.

"This isn't going to be easy," she mutters. Her stomach growls, and she claps a hand over it, cringing. "Ignore that."

I won't. I can't. How can I ignore the fact my mate is hungry and that I have the ability to earn a meal for her, if only we can solve this?

I trace my finger over the diagram, thinking hard. No one has ever accused me of being overly intelligent. In fact, very much the opposite.

"When I was on the streets, I was smart enough to make myself smaller, to do what I had to do to survive. I didn't start fights I couldn't finish, and I stayed away from those who were always looking to start one."

Ellison looks up from where she's examining the screens, a curious look on her face.

"I did not attend any of the fancy schools for the young in the capitol," I tell her by way of explanation. "These sort of logic problems, they wouldn't have fed me. I will, however, do my best to make sure you are fed tonight."

Her cheeks turn a bright pink, her eyes shining. Without a word, she walks around the table, cups my face in her hands, and pulls me down to plant a kiss on my lips.

It sets my soul on fire.

It also gets my cock incredibly hard, which is a distraction I don't need.

Not that I'm going to tell her to stop, not when her mouth meets mine like that.

"You are full of surprises, Ka-Rexsh," she says.

"So are you," I tell her, and I mean it.

"I hope we get that luxury tent." Ellison's teeth flash as she nibbles her lower lip.

"No matter what happens, I will ensure you are safe and comfortable this night, I promise you that."

Giving me a mystified look, she turns back to the screen.

I spend a moment just watching her. The beautiful slant of her cheekbones illuminated by the light of the fire, the warm brown of her eyes and the lush curve of her lips. She doesn't have horns, like a Draegon female would, but there is something delicate about her smooth forehead that makes me want to take care of her even more.

She is *mine*.

From the ragged, tangled ends of her silky brown hair to the dirty soles of her feet, Ellison is a dream come true. Capable, smart, brave and kind.

I want to give her everything she dreams for, from dinner and excellent sleeping accommodations to as many orgasms as her human body can take.

While I'm glad she's out of heat, and while I will never regret being able to please her last night, I wish it had been under different circumstances.

"I am sorry I was not able to court you as you deserve," I say out loud, surprising both of us. "I hope that you know, if circumstances were different, I would."

A finger twirls the ends of her hair, and she glances shyly up at me, through her dark lashes. It makes my breath catch, the flirtatiousness in that little look, the small smile dancing over her lips.

"There are reality shows on Earth, where they date different people. They aren't much different than this." She pauses, looking up at the night sky. "Well, other than the near-death experiences, and the flooding, and the blood, and the whole Ken thing. And usually the people know they're going on the shows and have time to prepare…"

"That is not the same as this at all," I tell her, not understanding her comparison.

"It is, though, because some of those couples, they end up falling in love. The show brings them together." She plops down on the ground, scratching out a rough diagram of the puzzle on the table into the dirt, working her way through multiple possibilities.

I watch her for too long, absorbed in the elegant way she uses her hands, the rise and fall of her pert breasts, the way her mouth moves as she thinks.

My attention finally switches back to the puzzle, and I draw multiple different lines, none of them correct.

This task is impossible. There is no way to solve it; either that, or I am as foolish as I feared.

Ellison even throws her hands up in frustration, sitting back, her legs splayed in front of her as she frowns down at her drawing in the dirt. Her wingless back heaves as she lets out a huge sigh. Her shoulders are so pretty. She has no wings, but I can be that for her.

I will show her how to fly.

"Five-minute warning," the alarm on the table intones, sounding exactly like Ken No Privates.

I'm still watching my mate.

Ellison is flightless, fangless, and her little fingers are soft and without talons.

All in all, she's defenseless, and used to seeing the world from one angle, from the ground.

"From the ground," I say out loud. "That's it."

"What's it?"

I register her question, that she has spoken, but my brain has finally caught up to the trick of this puzzle.

"We're looking at it wrong," I say out loud, talking at her excitedly. My wings flap slightly, and I hiss in dismay at the fresh wave of pain in the injured one. "The plane is the problem. It shouldn't be flat."

Out of my periphery, I see her shake her head in confusion.

Ellison asks something else, but I'm too busy. I have this. I can do it.

Carefully, I run the fingers of both hands across the screen, bringing them together.

The diagram distorts, now forming multiple planes.

"See? More than one level. That is how this puzzle is supposed to be solved." I'm grinning so wide my cheeks hurt, my heart pounding as I drag my finger across the now three-dimensional screen, the line following all the directions as I pull it through each opening.

Finally, I pull my hand away and wait, holding my breath.

The screen flashes green.

The clock stops at 2:11.

We solved it.

Ellison jumps up and down, wrapping her arms around me. "I know just how I want to celebrate," she says.

"I do too," I tell her, grabbing her hips and pulling her up to my waist.

She wraps her legs around me, careful not to kick my wings, and I meld my mouth to hers, savoring the perfect feel of her tongue, the delicious taste of her.

I don't need any other reward.

All I want is her.

CHAPTER
THIRTY-FIVE

ELLISON

Damn, Ka-Rexsh sure knows how to kiss.

My blood's on fire as I finally pull away, a little sheepishly, considering I basically jumped him. And I don't have heat to blame, like I did just yesterday.

I like him.

Maybe the idea of meeting a real love match on a reality show isn't far-fetched. Maybe this is just some weird story to tell our grandkids about how we met.

I stare up at him for a long time, taking in the proud set of his jaw, the curling horns protruding from his forehead, and the fiery orange of his eyes. He sure doesn't look like any of the guys in *World's Most Eligible*.

He does, however, look like he could be the romantic lead in a number of the alien fanfics I like to binge.

"We won," I make myself say, pumping my arms up

and down as Rex smiles at me. "You were brilliant. I never would have thought of that."

"I should have thought of it right away."

"How did you think of it?" I ask him.

"I was looking at you. You don't have wings. We all see the world one way at ground level. I realized I needed to look at the problem from a different level." He gives me that fangy grin, and he's so pleased with himself and just so damn cute that I want to kiss him again.

I really like him.

Suddenly, I throw my arms around myself, utterly self-conscious.

"What is it?" he asks.

"I'm not in heat anymore," I tell him quietly. I glance up to find him watching me with banked fire in his eyes. "But I still want you."

Something predatory sparks in that orange gaze.

And then Ken's hologram winks into view.

"Congratulations on winning another luxury challenge. You two sure are making everyone else look completely incompetent. This romance arc, though?"

Ken pinches his thumb and fingers together to make an extremely human chef's kiss.

"Your ratings are through the roof." The AI hologram turns to look at me. "By the way, I downloaded all the fanfics you bookmarked on your account. I'm reading them now."

"Oh," I say, at a loss. "You're going to love them." What else can I say to that?

"Behind you, your luxury accommodations for the

night. We will cut the feed in an hour so you have privacy. You can make whatever you would like to eat in the insta-pantry. Don't get too comfortable, though, because your cabin will disappear an hour after dawn. Early worm catches the bird!"

I nearly correct his idiom, but clamp my mouth shut at the last moment. No one likes a know-it-all, and I very much don't want to piss off Mr. No Privates.

Nope. If he wants the worm to catch the bird, so be it.

"Thank you," I tell him, beaming. If I beamed any harder, the hologram would need SPF. "Can you tell us if the crew is safe?"

But Ken winks out of existence, leaving my question hanging in the air and me alone with Rex.

The ground shakes and I squeak, grabbing Rex's arm to anchor myself.

In front of us, a round structure shoots out of the ground, a stone cottage of sorts—though it's unlike anything I've ever seen.

"I keep thinking nothing is going to surprise me, and then I keep getting proven wrong," I say.

Rex laughs. "There is much you haven't seen in this universe, but you are the only thing I care about seeing."

Aww. Good grief. "You sure know how to flirt." I squeeze his bicep a little, feeling warm all over, as Ken's words echo in my mind.

Privacy.

Ken said the cameras were going to be off in an hour.

"We're going to have privacy," I tell Rex.

"Good," Rex tells me, a mischievous smile on his face.

"I know what I want for dessert, and no insta-pantry can make it."

Whoooowhee. I fan myself, then stop, thinking hard.

"I don't know what an insta-pantry is," I admit.

Ka-Rexsh laughs and takes me by the hand. "Come with me, hyrulis. I will show you how the insta-pantry works, we will eat, and then, my Ellison, it will be my turn to feast."

I might not be in heat, but good grief, I'm hot all over.

It should be ridiculous, the way he says it, and if anyone else said something like that to me, I would absolutely be laughing.

But he's completely and utterly sincere, and it's refreshing to be with someone who says exactly what they want without any sort of subtext.

Rex clearly wants to eat me out, and I'd have to be half dead not to want him to do just that.

I'm not half dead.

CHAPTER
THIRTY-SIX

ELLISON

The tiny stone cottage is one of the strangest buildings I've ever been in. The rustic walls and wood beams seem like something out of a fairytale, whimsical and rough-hewn… and in complete contrast to everything inside.

Lights hang from the conical ceiling, and I stare at them in utter confusion.

They're not chandeliers, or bulbs, or anything I could possibly comprehend. The lights are fuzzy, and it's not because of my vision.

"Shoutout to the surgeon that did my Lasik, you're a real one, Dr. Adebayo." I scratch at my shoulder, still staring at the strange, fuzzy blob lights that seem to be suspended from fishing wire.

"I can't imagine having to do all this in glasses," I tell Rex.

"Glasses?" He frowns. "To drink from?"

"No, for my vision." I sigh. "Never mind. What are those things?"

"Some sort of light source," he answers, which is hardly illuminating.

Illuminating. Heh.

My stomach rumbles again, and Rex tugs me deeper into the little hut. The floor is sheathed in what seems to be stainless steel, as is all the furniture sitting beneath the strange lights.

While the shapes are vaguely familiar, it's like someone who'd never seen a chair or table before tried to build one based on a toddler's description.

I hold the tablet with one hand and cling to Rex with the other, hardly processing what I'm seeing.

Where did this come from? How is the AI just conjuring things from thin air, or the ground?

My brain understands that this so-called moon was once a giant, thriving space station. The weird furniture and floor must have once been in someone's home, or some building. Seeing it here, though, after surviving a flood with damned sea serpents in what looks like Baba Yaga's hut?

It's freaking weird.

"What do you want to eat?"

The question brings me back to the moment, and I take a minute to think on it. "Is it like… a set menu? How does it work?"

"You can scan through the options. There are thousands… but there are a few things it always makes better than others."

"What if you pick for me?" I ask, biting my lip. "Would you mind?"

The thought of having to make one more choice after today is too much. We are both alive. I'm exhausted.

And I'm hungry enough to eat just about whatever comes out of the box Rex is fiddling with. It reminds me of a microwave, though the door is on top and appears to screw into place.

Drooping, I plop onto one of the shiny metal chairs and wait.

"This has been a very weird experience," I finally say.

"I agree," Rex says, and though he's turned towards the insta-pantry where I can't see his face, he sounds like he's smiling.

"Not all bad, though," I amend hastily.

"I'm glad to hear that."

A second later, the insta-pantry dings, and Rex lifts the lid, pulling out a covered bowl. The aroma of cheese and herbs fills the small space, and my mouth waters automatically.

"This smells incredible," I say honestly, and he sets it in front of me with a grin.

"I'd rather hand-make it for you than use an insta-pantry, but I hope you like what I selected."

"What is it?" I ask, staring at the covered bowl with slight trepidation. I have no idea how to open it.

Noticing my confusion, Rex gently takes the bowl back, showing me a latch on the side. He presses it, and instead of the lid popping open, it simply folds into itself and vanishes.

I certainly wasn't expecting that.

From the top, he pulls off what can only be described as an alien spork and hands it to me.

"It is a protein and a carbohydrate, made with a vegetable sauce and cheese."

"Sounds appetizing," I manage, taking the hot bowl back from him.

A quick glance reveals something very familiar, though. It looks vaguely like lasagna.

While Rex selects something for himself from the insta-pantry, I poke at the meal with the spork. It smells good, sure, and I am hungry, but it is a little unsettling to eat a meal that just… magically appeared.

I eat it anyway.

And it's good.

"What do you think?" he asks, sitting across from me. Under the table, his tail wraps around my ankle, and I'm surprised by how sweet that bizarre contact feels.

"It reminds me of pasta with sun-dried tomatoes, but it's not quite that? It's weird because it's familiar but not like anything I've had all at the same time." I chew thoughtfully. Even the noodle-like sheet isn't quite the texture of lasagna. It's not bad.

I'm pretty sure I don't want to know what it's made of.

I'm hungry enough that I really don't care, either.

"I'm glad you're eating it. You need the calories."

I think that's the first time in my life a dude has told

me I need calories, and while he's not wrong, it makes me mad at all the other men I've ever dated.

Mad at them, and mad at myself for tolerating men who told me to eat less, talk less, make myself less.

Ka-Rexsh is nothing like that.

"You're a good one," I tell him suddenly, surprising both of us with the force of the words.

"You are a good one too," he replies, his tail tightening around my calf, his fangs showing as he smiles at me.

It's quiet, save for the sounds of us eating, and even the noise he makes chewing isn't offensive.

The bar, apparently, is in hell.

"I would consider this a third date, you know." It comes out of nowhere, and he pauses with his spork halfway to his mouth. I don't know what he picked to eat, but it's not the lasagna I'm eating.

"I do not know that we use the same calendar," Rex finally replies.

That makes me laugh, and I take another bite before continuing. "No, a date. It's what humans call, uh, the courtship period before you settle down with someone."

"Settle down?" His lip curls in disgust, showing fang, and it's so cute on him that I smile more broadly. "That is what humans call finding a partner? Settling down?"

"Sometimes," I answer cautiously. I don't want to shit all over the human race, and there's a pretty large amount of disdain in that question.

"Shouldn't it be settling up? Down seems so negative. I would think that you would not want to settle down."

I blink in surprise. He's not wrong—there is something… derogatory about that, but… "That's not what settle means. It means to like… calm down. Be calm."

"Nothing about starting a life with someone should change who you are, calm or not. Draegon are not perfect, but many of us, especially the Draegon of the village I was raised in, considered their partners, their mates, to be the ultimate achievement in life."

"I don't know." I poke at the remaining food. "I don't think people are achievements."

He frowns. "The word is not translating correctly. The mating partnership, maintaining it—it is not the result of some long pursuit, some ah, checking off a list of desirable traits found on a certain number of… interviews together." The word interview is pronounced very carefully, like he knows I might be offended by this and is trying to discuss it as delicately as he can.

I squirm, because I'm guilty of exactly that.

I have mentally cataloged all the things I like about him. All the things that I don't like, too—and I'm not sure that I know enough to know what I don't like about him.

"A true mating partnership…" He takes my hand in his, and I make myself look up at his earnest expression. "It is not about the individual qualities, bad or good. It is about supporting the whole of the partner, and lifting each other up. It is about making the world a better place, about being that person's home, their life support pod when their ship might fail."

"While the life support pod is a metaphor I'm not used to—"

He barks a laugh, and I grin at him.

"That sounds ideal," I finish.

"What were your parents like?" he asks.

Oh. He's told me what his are like, what he perceived his parents' and neighbors' relationships to be like.

"They were… distant. No unhappy, but maybe not necessarily happy, either." I frown, digging through my memories and trying to make sense of the emotions they dredge up. "They didn't talk about… things unless they were necessary." I'm struggling through the words. "They weren't mean to each other, or anything like that, but they seemed more like…" I push back my dirty hair, exhaling in frustration. "They seemed more like coworkers who had worked together for a long time than maybe even friends. They weren't interested in each other."

"What happened to them?" His question is soft, gentle.

"They divorced the summer I graduated from high school. It had been finalized for two days when the Roth attacked." My smile is bitter, and sadness threatens to steal my breath. "Maybe they would have both been happier alone, or with someone else, but that future was stolen from them. They both died in the first wave."

He squeezes my hand, and I look down, blinking back the stinging in my eyes. "Your planet had to grow up too fast," he says. "I think maybe you did, too."

I nod, unwilling to talk about this anymore.

It's unhealthy not to talk about the things that hurt us; I've been in enough on-again, off-again therapy sessions to know the truth of that.

I force another bite of the meal, though my appetite has waned, just to give myself something to do.

"My planet, on the other hand, is overgrown. Bloated, I would say. The monarchy is more greedy and power-hungry than ever, but the king has violated the most basic compact between ruler and ruled: he has simply stopped caring for them." He pauses, taking another bite, chewing fully before he continues. "It's treason to speak like this. No matter what happens here, I cannot go back home. I will not."

"Would you want to, if it were different?"

He gives me a long look. "I don't know that any of us can truly ever go home. I think that, ah, my home is no longer a place. I think my home could be a person."

My eyes go wide, and I turn to absolute mush.

In the space of a heartbeat, I've practically leapt across the table. He catches me in his arms, a rasping laugh on his mouth that I quickly replace with my lips.

He tastes like lemons and butter and, inexplicably, white wine, and he feels like he could be my home, too.

CHAPTER
THIRTY-SEVEN

KA-REXSH

Ellison is sunshine in human form. Her body is soft against mine, and I'm astonished by the fervor of her embrace.

She isn't in heat, and still, she chooses me.

She chooses this.

Finally, she pulls back, a self-deprecating smile on her face.

"I stink," she says, and the wrinkle in her nose paired with the frank admission makes me laugh.

"Luckily for you, I know how to take care of that particular problem."

"I don't want you to lick me clean," she says tartly.

A laugh booms out of me as I throw my head back. My wings rustle against the floor, pain shooting through the one still being repaired by the medical gel. "I was thinking a bath."

She balances on the tops of my legs, her arms thrown around my neck as she runs her fingers through my hair.

I could happily stay just like this the rest of the night, our arms around each other, the easy sound of her laugh tangled with mine.

"I don't see a bath anywhere in here. Is that another thing you can get out of the insta-pantry?"

"It will be on the underground floor."

"How do you know?" Her eyebrows quirk, her face so full of expression that I can almost hear the thoughts racing through her brain.

"This is modeled like a typical Cranyx home."

"Cranyx?" she asks, tripping over the word.

"Another species," I tell her. "They were… populous here."

Alarm bells sound, a klaxon in my mind—talking about the species who were on this station all those years ago feels like a very dangerous proposition. The station's sentience, the one Ellison named Ken, is surely listening in to all our conversations.

The being is not stable, or it would not have taken over this competition.

Bringing up the missing population won't help matters, of that much I'm sure.

"Come on," I tell her. "I will show you. The sleeping quarters are typically below ground, where the Cranyx are more comfortable. There will be a bath there as well."

"And no cameras," she says. "We'll be alone."

"That's what Ken No Privates said," I tell her seriously.

I hope the sentience was telling the truth, because what I have planned to help my Ellison relax tonight is just between me and her.

CHAPTER
THIRTY-EIGHT

ELLISON

The so-called bath is more like if a hot tub met an underground grotto.

Steam forms a cloud of vapor over the bubbling waters, and I stare at the bath, hewn out of rock, in complete disbelief.

The air down here, in the underground level, is colder than above, and the steaming waters sound like the perfect way to unwind.

I don't even think about it. I don't even pause to consider anything other than how badly I want to get in that tub and get clean and relax.

I strip the filthy clothes off me in a matter of seconds, then scramble over to the rough stone steps and submerge as quickly as I can.

It's blissfully quiet and hot under the surface, and I'm immediately soothed.

When I surface, Rex hasn't moved from the bottom of the stairs.

He looks shell-shocked, and I tilt my head, trying to figure out what's wrong with him.

"What is it?" I ask in a hushed voice.

I thought I was all out of adrenaline, but the sight of him, so still—it freaks me right out.

"You are the most desirable female I have ever laid eyes upon. I would have thought I was sated after last night; I thought I could lie to myself about not needing you again, but right now? Right now I do not even want that water to touch your skin. I want all of you to myself."

Oh, is that all?

A slow smile turns up the corners of my cheeks. "You scared me."

His eyes narrow, and his shoulders slump slightly. "I promise you I can practice self-control."

I stand up, the water coming up to just beneath the curve of my breasts.

His throat bobs.

"I wasn't asking for self-control. I thought something was wrong."

He says something in a low tone that doesn't translate, and then he's half running, half flying towards me. His pants hit the floor, and when I blink, he's next to me again, wings spread high over the water.

Everything about him feels good, feels right, and the desire welling inside me comes as a slight surprise.

"I like you," I tell him, running a thumb over his temple, then tracing the base of one of his horns.

"And I like you, Ellison of Earth," he says, so serious that it makes my heart stutter. His tail wraps around just beneath my knees, and he cradles my head and tilts it back, like he's going to dip and kiss me.

He dunks me under the water before I can so much as swoon, and I come up laughing and sputtering.

"That was not nice," I say to him, but I'm cackling, which minimizes the impact of my words considerably.

"Just wanted to make sure you were ready to be soaped," he says easily, grabbing one of the stone canisters that line the edge of the tub.

I hadn't even noticed them.

He scoops out a dollop of herb-scented cream, then plops it on my head.

"Hey, I can do that—" My words are cut off by a low moan.

"I know you can," he says with a laugh. "But isn't this much more fun?"

My eyes nearly cross as he massages the stuff into my hair, the tips of his talons scraping deliciously along my scalp.

"I can agree with that," I finally answer.

"Mmmm, I thought you might," he says, continuing to soap me all over.

When he sets me on the edge of the tub, spreading my legs apart, I'm as limp as a fresh noodle from the instapantry from the massage and the heat of the water.

"Am I allowed to have a taste?" he asks, an eyebrow arched.

"Only if I get to hold your horns like handlebars." I wink.

He tips his head back and laughs, pushing my thighs apart. "That is a very specific request."

"I'm just trying to live my fanfic heroine dreams," I tell him, grinning.

Has it ever been this fun with a partner? Have I ever made another man laugh, have I ever wanted to?

I'm not sure.

And when he sets his tongue between my legs, I might just forget my entire name.

CHAPTER THIRTY-NINE

ELLISON

The next day comes too early.

I'm sore.

Sore from the athletic requirements of the previous day's trials, and sore from Ka-Rexsh's bedroom skills, too.

Not in a bad way, though—it's a sort of delicious tenderness that reminds me I had a really good time with him.

A really, really good time with him.

"You're smiling," he says. His lips brush against mine, his fang snagging on my bottom lip, followed by his tongue lapping at the spot. "Does that mean you're happy? You did not give me your high five last night, so I wasn't sure if I had earned it well enough."

That has me opening my eyes wider, and I stifle a yawn. "What?"

"The high five."

I inspect his face for signs that he's joking around, but he doesn't so much as blink, which is a bit creepy.

"Does the high five not mean you were pleased with my sexual prowess? Is it not how you show your sexual partner that they brought you pleasure?"

"Ah." I clear my throat. "Well. It doesn't mean that all the time."

How the hell am I supposed to get myself out of this one?

"I can see I misunderstood," he says, and there's a hint of coldness that surprises me.

"Hey," I say, putting my hands on either side of his face. "Don't be upset, it was a misunderstanding. I will high five you if you really want that, but it doesn't have some deep meaning."

He inhales, nostrils flaring, gaze darting between my eyes.

I continue on, since he doesn't seem to be calming down just yet. "If you want, I can show my appreciation another way."

A terrible, silly part of me wants to hold up both hands and teach him about a double high five, but I don't. I just wait.

"How?" He cocks his head.

"May I touch you?" I ask, and it comes out a lot sultrier than I expected.

He swallows, then nods. "My body is yours to do what you will with."

So instead of giving him a high five, I kiss my way down his body, inspecting every muscle, every scar.

"That one is from an accident with a halvek."

I kiss the raised edge of the scar, then run a fingertip along it. "What's a halvek?"

"A large animal. Livestock." His voice is strained, and I smile, loving that I can make him sound like that.

"Mmm," I say, continuing my path down his body. Last night was about me, and then we curled up together and slept.

I want to make him feel good.

I want him to know that I care about how he feels, too.

High five or not.

His hand fists in my hair, and I finally get down to the prize—that thick alien cock. It's already hard, and I watch it move as I run my hand idly up and down it.

Moisture and heat pool between my legs because I already know how damned good Rex feels inside me.

Like this, though, eye-to-eye with it, it's pretty intimidating.

"This, what your dick is doing… it's called what?" I ask him, then lick the tip of it, causing him to hiss and groan before I get an answer.

"I'm going to come before you get on top of me if you keep that up," he says with a groan. His talons tickle my scalp, reminding me of the wonderful way he washed my hair last night, the way he took care of me.

"Maybe that's what I want." I give him my most devious grin.

"It's called skithing," he manages. It sounds like sky-thing, and it makes no sense to me.

Can't say I'm surprised there isn't a translation.

Dicks don't do that back home, that's for damn sure.

Not that I'm complaining. My body tightens up in anticipation, and I have half a mind to hop on top and have some fun.

But no.

I want to show him that I'm pleased with him, and I've never had anyone turn down a good old-fashioned blow job.

He is definitely the first I've been with who didn't demand one, though.

I lick up and down, working up the courage to put my mouth around him. When I finally do, Rex is tense all over, his thigh muscles standing out and his stomach twitching in anticipation.

"Fuck, hyrulis, you tease me with your wicked mouth."

I bob up and down, trying to get used to the strange sensation of a pulsing dick—but I must be a coward because it's... well, it's just not for me.

His cock leaves my mouth, and I wipe my lips with the back of my hand. "I can't get you off like that—I'm not used to the skithing thing. I could get used to it, though."

"Good," Rex tells me, his fingers gripping my hips and pulling me upright. "I want to come deep inside you. It's where I belong, and you know it too, even if you don't want to admit it yet, my Ellison."

With that, he lines himself up with me and I slam down, then luxuriate in the delicious feel of him. Whatever the skithing is, it feels much better on my G-spot than my uvula or whatever.

The longer we tangle together, sweaty and breathless, the more I think he might be right.

He might have a point about belonging there, because I've never felt this good in my entire life.

In that moment right before orgasm, as my body builds closer and closer to release, I see it all with a clarity that I'm sure later I'll blame on hormones—but I can see it.

I can see a future with Ka-Rexsh.

It's full of laughter, and comfort, and pleasure, and safety.

And partnership.

He could be a partner, and so much more.

The orgasm rips through me at the same time as that epiphany, and I sag against him, exhausted and happy and nervous all at once.

I like Ka-Rexsh, and I'm pretty sure I could love him, too.

Possibilities run through my head as he runs his hand down my bare back and over the thick curve of my ass.

"I like every bit of you, but this part," he squeezes, and I laugh. "This part is my favorite, I think."

My alien is an ass man. Who would have thought?

I smile broadly at him, and he returns it, kissing the tip of my nose, then my mouth.

The comms tablet chimes where we set it to charge last

night. Rex pulls away from me slowly, and I sluggishly roll from the low platform of the bed, his release still hot and dripping from within me.

"I'm going to have to clean up before I can answer that," I tell him.

He smirks from the bed, the low pre-dawn light filtering in through the tiniest of windows just above ground level, casting him in greys and greens.

"You're beautiful," I tell him.

"You honor me," he says, the smirk replaced by solemnity. A hand settles over his heart, talons missing on all five of his fingers now.

The sight—and knowledge of the reason why they're gone—makes me blush, and I clamber into the pool before I get any more embarrassed.

Or worse, I say the words on the tip of my tongue. It's too soon to tell him I might love him.

It can't be love. Not yet.

———

By the time I've cleaned up, it's past dawn, and the underground sleeping area's bathed in a golden light. Rex follows me into the tub, and I'm tempted to slap his butt, but I know if I touch him like that again, we'll just end up in each other's arms all over again.

I'm trusting the AI's word that we've had privacy so far, but I don't doubt the minute our deal is up from the reward challenge, we'll be streamed everywhere again.

Regardless of any compromising positions we might find ourselves in.

Regretfully, I towel off with the seemingly endless supply of towels next to the rock-hewn tub.

"Oh my god," I say out loud, staring at where my clothes fell the previous night. "You've got to be kidding me."

"What's wrong?" Ka-Rexsh is next to me in a flash, dripping all over the polished rock floor.

"My clothes." I point, and for some reason, I'm hit with the uncontrollable urge to laugh. "This isn't funny," I wheeze, and all I can think is that my body is getting rid of the excess adrenaline through my funny bone. "I'm sorry," I say.

Bending over, I grab the clothes off the chair.

Sometime in the night, yesterday's clothes were taken.

And replaced with a set of extremely familiar pajamas. My pajamas, to be exact, though dirt- and hole-free, as if they were painstaking recreated.

Maybe they were.

I sink to the floor in my towel, dumbfounded and staring at the clothes with my mouth hanging wide open.

"I don't like what this might mean."

"You're right to worry," Rex tells me, a heavy hand on my shoulder.

I reach up and squeeze it, thankful for the small comfort of his touch.

"Most men would tell me there is nothing to worry about," I blurt.

"I'm not most men. I think this means that Ken No Privates is up to something."

"Or he just liked watching me in my pajamas," I venture. Rex using the very formal name of Ken No Privates isn't quite as funny as it was yesterday.

"That might be worse."

"It might be," I agree.

The comms tablet chimes again, and I shimmy into the clean clothes, grateful at least that the thick sports bra and underwear are also there. Going braless on this ghost alien space station sounds positively horrible.

The hairs stand up on the back of my arms, and I squeeze my eyes tight, trying not to panic as memories of yesterday morning's near-death experiences wash over me.

How was that only a day ago?

It feels like a lifetime ago.

"I want to get out of here," I finally say through gritted teeth.

"We will," Rex says quietly, still hovering beside me. "We will."

Blowing out a long breath, I force myself to calm down. One of my therapists taught me that trick after the Roth attack, and though it doesn't always help, it does now.

In and out, I focus on the feeling of the air filling my lungs, my diaphragm, imagine it carrying life-giving oxygen to every finger on my hand, every toe on my foot.

I am alive.

I am sore, but uninjured.

. . .

I'm not alone.

I am not alone.

"I will keep you safe, hyrulis," he says, as if he's reading my thoughts.

I open one eye, and he's crouched in front of me, a worried expression on his face.

"I know you will," I tell him. It's true. I know he will do his best.

At some point along the way, I chose to trust him.

Now, I'm sure I can.

He helps me to my feet, and I finally pick the comms tablet off the top of the small table I set it on last night.

A quick look tells me the chat's been active while Rex and I were... also, ahem, active.

> Selene: We had some trouble at dusk
>
> Selene: Did you all get reward challenges
>
> Lucy: Oh we got one. We did not win it.
>
> Lily: We did
>
> Poppy: We had some trouble too
>
> Poppy: I'm using the word trouble very, very loosely

I keep scrolling. I missed a lot. Anything that might have details in it is blacked out.

"It's weird, right?" I ask Rex. "All the censored messages. Ken really doesn't want us to meet up with the other couples, it seems like. Anything that might give away where they are... he's just blacked it out."

"Created sentient beings like Ken have their own reasoning, and often it has nothing to do with the way you or I would reason." Rex does look troubled by it, his gaze far away.

"I mean, it must have to do with the way he wants to run the show, right? Like, he is keeping us separate for a reason. Maybe it's just for the, uh," my brain stumbles over the word I want. "Story arcs."

"Maybe," Rex concedes, but he doesn't look convinced.

> Selene: We made it through the night

Made it through the night? I cringe, feeling something that must be akin to survivor's guilt. Hell, maybe it *is* survivor's guilt.

> Lucy: So did we
>
> Lily: We're good here too
>
> Poppy: Same.
>
> Poppy: Anyone heard from Ell?
>
> Lucy: Is anyone else still in heat
>
> Lucy: It's horrible
>
> Lucy: I'm considering banging him just to feel better

I pause the message I'd been tapping out, completely

thrown by Lucy's. I don't know why I didn't stop to consider they were probably all in heat and struggling with it. It didn't even occur to me that they:

1. were also in heat
2. were likely feeling horrible because of point number one
3. weren't in love with their partners

Which leads me to point four: I am falling in love with Ka-Rexsh

It's funny how it bubbles up to my consciousness fully now, the truth of it.

"Are you going to tell them you are safe, hyrulis?" Ka-Rexsh prods, a quizzical look on his face. His tail wraps around my ankle, an alien gesture that makes me feel warm and fuzzy inside all the same.

> Ellison: We're safe

I bite my lip. It feels wrong to tell them we won the luxury reward challenge. It would feel even worse to not tell them I'm not in heat.

> Ellison: Rex and I mated. I'm not in heat

Lucy: Holy shit Ell are you okay

Lily: I'll come find him and kill him if I have to

> Ellison: I'm better than okay

> Ellison: It was my choice, and I have no regrets

Lucy: Once again, and I cannot emphasize this enough, holy shit. You are the queen of regret when it comes to men. Are you okay?

Lily: I would ask if you've been abducted by aliens, but uh...

Selene: Congratulations

Selene: Whatever you do, don't go back to their planet with him

"That's ominous," I say out loud.

Selene: That is, if you get off this one

Right. Let's borrow *that* trouble. Sheesh. Selene is a real ray of sunshine. I frown, thinking it over. How the hell would she know enough about the Draegon to advise me not to go back to their planet?

Weird.

Lily: It's a space station, not a planet

Poppy: I think our next challenge is starting. Be safe. Check in tonight.

The ground rumbles, and Rex grips my arm to keep me from falling, his tail still anchoring my leg.

"We better get up there," I tell him.

"You are upset. Which of them upset you?" He narrows his eyes at me.

"We can talk about it later. The earthquake shit is freaking me out. Can we go upstairs?"

"I do not understand what earthquakeshit is."

I don't bother answering—I'm throwing on my boots which, blessedly, weren't stolen with the rest of the comfortable hiking clothes.

I might be in my damned pajamas, but I'm not barefoot.

Thank Ken No Privates for small miracles, I guess.

I clutch the tablet to my chest, and Rex grabs the rest of our belongings and helps me hustle up the narrow stone stairs.

"I should have fed you before now," he growls, his wings twitching in irritation.

"You need food too," I tell him.

He sprints for the insta-pantry, and it dings as his fingers fly across the screen. Whatever he programmed into it didn't need a whole lot of time to make.

I have a feeling it's not going to be alien lasagna.

Dust fills the air, and I cough as the little hut continues to shake. My feet are braced a bit wider than my hips, and I have one arm outstretched just so I don't lose my balance and eat dirt. The formerly polished surface of the alien hut's now covered in clods of dirt, and I pull the neckline of the pajama shirt over my face to avoid inhaling space station dust.

I'm quite sure I don't want that in my lungs, thank you very much.

Thankfully, the insta-pantry chimes nearly right away, and Ka-Rexsh scoops whatever he ordered out and drags me outside.

Not a minute too soon, too, seeing as how the hut starts to cave in on itself right away.

Ken appears a second later, and I shriek at the hologram's sudden appearance.

"I don't think that's a normal good morning, Miss Price, even for a human." Ken glares at me, like my shriek of utter terror ruined whatever greeting he had planned.

"I trust you slept well, contestants?" he finally asks.

Rex hands me half of what looks like a protein bar, and I shove it in my mouth instead of answering. Calories are important.

Especially considering I have no idea when we'll get to eat again.

"Since you two have successfully completed two challenges I've put before you, and because you placed first in the childish performance the, ah, former producers arranged for you, I've decided that you two have made it to the fast track."

Does that math add up? I'm not sure.

"Fast track?" I try to repeat. My teeth are stuck together thanks to the protein bar. It tastes like bananas and pineapple and, strangely, peanut butter.

I'm doing my best not to think about what it tastes like at all, actually.

"Yes. You two are the only mated pair, and for whatever reason, the audience reaction isn't nearly as good as it is for our remaining unmated couples. I suppose the tension is gone. You two work well together."

Ken announces this with the air of someone who has been fully deprived of seeing us suffer.

I decide that Ken isn't my favorite non-person person.

It doesn't matter that he's the only non-person person I know.

"What does fast track mean?" Rex asks, his tail tight around my ankle.

"It means, my surly Draegon friend, that today's challenge will be your last! Because I'm sick of you two."

"Rude," I tell Ken. I make a face and bite off another chunk of the godawful protein bar.

"Would you prefer to continue to compete, Ellison Price?" Ken's hologram eyes seem to glow.

"No, Ken, I would not," I make myself say. "If you want us to win the competition, that's fine by me."

"Oh, don't be so hasty, Ellison." Ken smiles, and I step back.

His teeth aren't right. They're pointy. Pointy, and there's too many of them, like the AI had no idea how to make teeth look right.

The overall effect is truly freakish.

"Uncanny valley, much?" I mutter.

"Today's challenge is unlike any the two of you have faced so far."

Rex reaches for my hand, but the hologram raises one finger, shaking it at him like he's a naughty child. "Ah-ah!"

We both freeze.

Literally.

I try to blink, but I can't move.

"There. Today's challenge, your final challenge, your capstone assignment, your senior reality thesis—"

I glare at Ken, and he narrows his eyes at me, pausing before he picks up his speech again.

"Will be conducted separately. The challenge is simple. Find your way back to each other. When you find each other, the challenge is complete, and you will be rewarded."

No. I don't want to be separated from Rex. We're supposed to be together.

No.

I don't want to do this alone!

Ken claps his hands.

Whatever I want doesn't matter because when I'm finally unstuck and able to blink, Rex is nowhere to be found.

I'm alone.

CHAPTER FORTY

KA-REXSH

My mate is gone.

A roar bursts out of me, and I sink to my knees, overcome.

For a long while, it's the only thought in my mind, fear for her and anger the only emotions I'm capable of.

Sitting here isn't going to get me back to her, though, so I stand up, rage making my wings flare out and my muscles twitch. I will find my mate.

My Ellison.

I take my new location in, along with a deep breath.

A mistake, because my rage means the mechanism for fire deep in my chest triggers. I do not want to change—breathing fire right now would be a mistake, one that could be deadly for me and for my mate.

I force calm.

Force oxygen into my bloodstream.

Force the building fire in the specialized part of my anatomy to calm.

To wait.

I will have use for it soon—but not yet.

First, I must find her.

My Ellison.

My future.

My home.

CHAPTER
FORTY-ONE

ELLISON

"Well, this fucking sucks," I say, scratching at a new bug bite on my neck. I've been slogging through marshy terrain for the last hour at least.

Honestly, I have no idea how much time has actually passed because the damn comms tablet winked out of my grasp when my boy Ken beamed me out to wherever the hell I am now. My hand shields my eye from the glare, and I look up, trying to judge it. The sun is in a different position in the sky.

Revealing that time has, in fact, passed. Shocking, truly. I sigh, smacking at an overly large winged bug.

"Gross." I stare at the thing, easily the size of a hummingbird, though it looks like a mosquito. That nasty critter would take a pint of my blood at once. A phlebotomist's dream.

"I miss Ka-Rexsh."

It's not the first time I've said it, and it won't be the last.

Mud sucks at my feet with each step I take, and insects buzz around my head at an absolutely infuriating pitch. It's humid, too, like all the water that flooded the path yesterday has gone airborne.

"Walking in a summer-soupy maze," I sing. A winter wonderland would be preferable, but my odds for surviving snow in my shortie pajamas would be decidedly lower.

I stop, wide-eyed, at that thought. No, not the snow thought, the other one.

A maze.

That's what this is—a maze of some sort. I look around, craning my head so fast I almost pull a muscle in my neck.

Shit. Mazes in reality shows aren't ever straightforward.

"Christ on a bike," I mutter, groaning at my own unintentional pun.

If I'm right, and this is a maze—and considering that big tree to my right is looking pretty damn familiar, I'm pretty sure I'm right—this is basically going to be a multi-challenge bonanza.

And I don't have my partner with me.

"Competitors, you have now been in the labyrinth for thirty minutes." Ken's voice booms out, and I wince. Even the giant mosquitoes seem offended. "Your difficulty level will scale up every thirty minutes. Once you find each other, or the middle of the maze, your challenge is completed."

"Shit." Every thirty minutes? I'm doomed.

Cubicle life and a steady of diet of Girl Scout cookies and chips has not prepared me well for this moment.

"The good news is I'll be out fast. The bad news is, this is going to hurt." The mosquitoes don't seem to care about this announcement.

"You will each be provided a weapon with which to protect yourself."

"Damn, Ken, you don't have to sound so happy about it." The fucker sounds positively gleeful at the idea of us having to be armed. Good grief.

I don't think I've ever seen a reality show in which the contestants were armed for PROTECTION. I sigh, glaring at the nearest mosquito.

"I will shoot you," I tell it pathetically.

The ground rumbles, and I hold back a yawn.

It's a close call. I'm both tired physically and tired of Ken's drama. Still, I have a feeling I don't want the AI to think I'm bored. The last thing I want is more drama because I made a bad choice to pick at the sentient space station system software.

"Two wrongs don't make a right," I say primly.

The mosquitoes remain unimpressed.

I stand there for a little longer, wondering if Ken's done giving his enthusiastic doom-and-gloom instructions, then tug at my leg in an attempt to get myself unstuck from the thick mud.

Finally, with a loud squelch, my foot comes free—but not before I'm splattered in the sticky, foul stuff.

The ground rumbles again, and I glance around because now I know that means Ken is changing something up here in alien reality TV hell. Sure enough, a thunderous noise fills my head, and I clap my hands over my ears reflexively.

Pumpkin shit pie, I need that weapon, and I need it now, because whatever is making that noise must be fucking huge.

And I sincerely doubt that noise is saying, "I want to be friends, come out and play!"

Well, maybe it is, but if that is what that noise means, it's lying.

I do not like this, nope, I do not like this at all.

"Weapon, weapon, I need a weapon," I chant, like that's going to make one magically appear.

No sooner has that thought flitted in and out of my head than something rockets to the ground in front of me, sending more thick mud splattering all over me.

A clump slides down my face, and I approach the object cautiously because I wouldn't put it past Ken to just drop a giant hungry ant right in front of me.

Today's theme: killer bugs.

I regret thinking that immediately. I don't think Ken can read my mind... but also... maybe he can. Who's to say?

Certainly not I.

Trepidatious, I finally get close enough to see the object sinking into the disgusting muck.

"Oooh," I breathe, thrilled for a beat, at least until I remember that I'm going to have to actually use it, and accurately, at that.

It's a bow and a quiver full of arrows.

Sure, I haven't practiced archery since I was about thirteen, but I wasn't the blue-ribbon winner that summer for nothing.

"Like riding a bike," I murmur, then play tug-of-war with the mud for the bow and quiver until they finally jerk free.

Momentum sends me directly onto my ass into the slop, and I swear, sweat is rolling between my boobs.

I'm intensely aware of the fact I smell like an onion, but as that clicking sounds again, so loud I wince, I decide caring at all about the way I smell and look is stupid. I need to get somewhere safe, and I need to find Rex as soon as possible. I don't want to think about what Ken considers a challenge as more thirty-minute increments stack up.

By the time I get out of the mud, I'm pretty much coated in it.

"Maybe I have to fight a giant man-eating worm that hunts on scent alone," I say, then laugh, because that's the plot of one of the most popular books on Earth.

I cringe. Damn.

I really hope I don't have to fight a giant worm. "No thank you on the worms, Ken, I'll pass."

The quiver goes over my shoulder, the strap nestling between my breasts, and I hang the bow over a shoulder, too. I pull one of the arrows out, then tilt my head as I inspect it.

"Camp Ozarka never had any arrows like this." It's alien, that's for sure. Instead of a pointed tip, or a suction cup, like what the littlest campers used, it's got a heavy round end.

I have no idea how this thing is going to fly, and my original enthusiasm at being gifted a weapon I actually know how to use goes out the window.

It's been well over a decade since I last used a bow and arrow, so the odds were already not great, but an arrow like this, with a cylinder on the end? I have no idea what to do with it.

Shrugging, I keep moving through the marsh, trying to avoid going in a circle.

Again.

Problem is, every step I take seems to take me closer to the loud crunching and clicking. Dread pools in my stomach, and I wish, for the hundredth time, that Ka-Rexsh was with me.

I hope he's safe. I hope he's having a better time than I am, because if anyone can survive this type of thing, it's him. I've been lucky to have him in my corner this whole time, and when I get to see him again, I'm going to give him a million high fives.

And maybe a blow job.

Who could say?

I'm so involved in my little Ka-Rexsh reunion fantasy that I don't realize the stalks in front of me aren't cattails until I'm right up on them.

They're not waving in the non-existent breeze, like my brain tried to tell me, but I was so wrapped up in imagining my alien mate's hot bod that I didn't notice there wasn't a breeze at all.

Fuck. Me.

The ground shifts, mud oozing towards the stalks, which are waving frantically, and each at least the size of my arm.

"I don't have a good feeling about this," I moan, the mud sucking me towards the dancing stalks.

Not stalks, antennae.

"Oh, you wanted a fucking worm?" I yell at myself, slapping a bug on my bicep, then pulling the bow out.

One of the arrows follows, and I frown in chagrin at the weird-ass weapon.

Then I try to back the fuck up because whatever this thing is, it's huge.

"Not a fucking worm," I yell, the mud sucking at me, the animal in front of me drawing me deeper as it rises out of the muck.

The heinously loud clicking sounds again, and I look left as I scramble backwards.

It's so enormously large that my brain doesn't comprehend what it is at first. Red-brown chitinous pebbled exoskeleton rises higher, two elements clacking together.

A pincer.

"Not a fucking worm!" I yell again, throwing my hands in the air in absolute irritation. "Couldn't be something squishy, nope."

A crab? What the hell is it?

"Oh, you wanted a worm? Fuck you!" I mimic Ken, putting one hand on my hip.

Apparently, I've lost my mind.

My gaze darts right, only to see another enormous claw.

Then I look straight ahead, the clicking sounding somehow frustrated now. The mud is sucking at the huge animal, too, and it's not happy about it.

Its eye is four times the size of my head. Well, at least *that* part of it is squishy. I scrabble backwards, losing my balance again and landing on my butt.

"Holy fucking shit," I breathe as its legs appear, coated in muck. "Crawfish."

It finishes freeing itself from the marsh, looming over me. It's the size of my apartment building, or close to it. Not that I'm a great judge of size. I'm more of an eyeball it, close enough kind of girl.

"Crawfish intensifies," I say weakly.

I don't think I'm going to make it past the first challenge.

CHAPTER
FORTY-TWO

KA-REXSH

When nothing shoots me out of the sky, I decide Ken No Privates might not be as evil or unstable as I first supposed. The weapon he saw fit to provide me with upon announcing the difficulty increase is strapped to my hand, fitted over my fingers, a metal replacement for the talons I bit off.

A Draegon is already weapon enough.

My wings ache already, unused to this sort of sustained flight. The drop from the ship onto the surface of the moon was one thing, but a marathon of search and rescue requires a different type of musculature.

My people have grounded me for far too long.

My injured wing hurts particularly badly, and I grit my teeth.

It doesn't matter how badly it hurts.

I have to get to my little human mate. She is soft and vulnerable and not bred to fight, nor has she any experience.

Ken must want us to reunite and fight together, for whatever twisted reason.

I will not pretend to understand the motivations of the space station's sentience—I can only hope that Ellison and I are well and truly gone from the surface of this place before it tires of us.

At least it's moved us on to this final challenge, a maze of epic proportions. Even from my altitude, I'm sickened by the sheer size of it. It would take us days to travel to the center, and I've been in the air for a solid forty-five minutes now without sighting Ellison.

Pain jolts up my wing, the muscle seizing up from either lack of use or the serpent's efforts yesterday morning.

I will not let it take me down.

Being on land, in that maze, means hours upon hours lost without Ellison, and I refuse to put her through that.

She needs me.

The entire side of my body shakes with effort as I continue flying, scouring the maze below for any sign of her.

In the distance, an explosion sounds, a deafening boom that makes me snarl.

I know, without a doubt, that my mate is in trouble.

I fly faster.

CHAPTER
FORTY-THREE

ELLISON

Smoke billows beside the kaiju crawfish, the heat blistering my face. From the smell, I'm pretty sure I singed my eyebrows off.

"Well, that's not what I planned on happening." I blink, staring at the resulting fire from the arrow gone wide.

Explosive arrows, apparently.

I cringe because I've already fallen on them once

I'm pretty sure I do not want to land on my back.

"Ellison barbecue is very much not on the to-do list." I tilt my head. "It could be on the crawfish's to-do list, but it's not on mine. Just FYI, Ken No Privates."

I think I might be in shock.

The crawfish does its weird little clicky thing, staring at the flames in the remnants of the trees next to it.

"I don't think I can eat seafood again," I manage.

Do I dare try to shoot another arrow at it? I missed pretty badly, and I banged up my arm when I let the string go.

It slapped me silly, and is probably why the arrow went wide.

A welt's already forming on the inside of my arm, and I wince at the thought of aiming badly enough again to hurt it worse.

Then a claw slams down in front of me, and I decide that getting eaten by a swamp lobster is a worse fate than having a painful bruise.

"Here goes nothing," I say, nocking an arrow and aiming carefully, trying to remember all the shit my camp counselors drilled into me all those summers ago.

The arrow flies when I loose the string, and while it does hit my arm, it doesn't slap it nearly as hard.

The arrow explodes on the side of the crawfish's face, a massive show of red and orange fireworks… that do absolutely nothing.

The crawfish screams, enraged.

Did you know crawfish could scream? I didn't.

Did you know all those little legs can move pretty quick when they want to?

I'm not a fan.

"I didn't know I needed crustacean-related nightmare fuel, but I guess I'll be lucky to have a nightmare, after this." I don't know who I'm talking to, but it helps me feel slightly better to say it.

A massive shadow passes over me, blocking out the

scorching sun, and a fresh wave of fear sends a chill down my spine.

Have thirty minutes already passed? Is the next threat aerial?

I nock another arrow, ready to fight for my life—then release it, sobbing, as Ka-Rexsh lands in front of me like an avenging dragon angel.

He takes me in his arms, and I cry like an idiot. "There's a giant kaiju crawfish and I hurt my arm," I try to tell him, wriggling so I can get space to fire another shot.

But it's not there.

Or rather, we're not there. The maze is gone.

Alas, poor labyrinth, I hardly knew ye.

An icy wind sweeps over me, such a stark contrast to the heat of the marsh that I shiver all over.

"I found you," Rex tells me, holding my muddy face in his hands. He kisses me, hard, and I melt into him, beyond relieved.

Relieved to be in his arms, relieved that he found me—and relieved that it's him.

"My Ka-Rexsh," I say, pulling away, my gaze tracing over every inch of his face, checking him for wounds. I hug him close again.

He's okay.

He's here, he's real, and he's okay.

I'm crying again.

"As touching as this is, I have to break you up so we can continue with our show format," a familiar voice says.

"Ken?" I glance around. "Is the crawfish okay?"

It's an utterly absurd thing to ask, but I feel bad for the kaiju crustacean.

Ken stares at me for a long moment, apparently thrown.

I swallow.

"The crawfish, as you call it, is fine."

"Thank you," I say meekly, vowing not to interrupt Ken again. He looks less transparent here, wherever here is.

It looks like a sci-fi rendering of a spaceship. Bright white lights, a huge screen full of symbols I can't make heads or tails of, and a whole lot of shiny metal.

"As I was saying," Ken continues slowly, smiling expansively at us, "You two are the first to finish your journey here on *Mated and Afraid*. As such, you will be the first to arrive at the Suevan colony that Billie and Ayro worked so hard to help secure for you all."

"Are Billie and Ayro there?" I interrupt.

So much for that resolution.

Ken's grin falters. A second ticks by. Another.

"Sorry," I say, only slightly sorry. Rex tightens his grip on my waist.

"Billie and Ayro are none of your concern," he finally answers. "But you will find out everything soon, when you tune in to another episode of *Mated and Afraid* yourselves. In addition to the incredible prize package your former producers put together, I also arranged for a basket of goodies to help you remember your time here on Station X0-3. And you, at home, can purchase it too!"

Ken addresses this to what I can only assume is one of the camera feeds. "Join us again for another episode of *Mated and Afraid*, where we will find out if Lily and Zan-De'Eer will fare any better against my labyrinth!"

Ken's smile fades.

Suddenly, I wish I were facing the crawfish again because Ken is fucking scary. I cling to Rex, and he wraps his wing around me, hiding me from view.

"I'll be transferring you to Sueva momentarily," Rex says, his over-the-top announcer voice replaced by something more matter-of-fact.

"What happened to—"

Rex coughs, cutting off my question and giving me a meaningful look.

"My comms tablet?" I finish meekly. I was going to ask what happened to all the people on the space station, because it's important.

It's not right for thousands of living beings to just disappear in the blink of an eye.

"I've sent the comms tablet ahead with your branded merchandise," Ken says. "Now close your eyes. You might see a bright light, but this shouldn't hurt one bit."

Rex folds me into his body as soon as Ken finishes that sentence, pressing my face against his chest, wings cocooning me.

If there's a bright light, there's not a crawfish's chance in hell he's going to risk me seeing it.

When he finally releases me, I'm dizzy.

I plop down on the floor, and dried mud flakes off my legs.

"Holy shit." A woman who glows like Tinkerbell crouches before me. "Kanuz, look, it's the couple from *Mated and Afraid*. The AI kept its word."

"Are you a fairy?" I ask her, woozy.

"Fucking hell," the blonde woman rolls her eyes. "No. I'm Gen, and you're on Sueva. You're going to be alright."

I exhale, and then I promptly and quietly pass out.

CHAPTER
FORTY-FOUR

ELLISON

Rex is holding me.

That's the first thing I'm aware of.

"Where are we?" I ask him, muzzy.

"Ellison, you scared me." He holds me tighter.

"I told you she was fine, you big bat." A curly-haired woman rolls her eyes in my direction. "These aliens are so overbearing. I'm Tati, I'm a doctor. How are you feeling?"

"Fine," I say automatically, then take a second and do a mental survey of all my body parts. Intact. "Tired," I amend. "What happened?"

"Well, as far as we can tell," the glowing woman answers, "you have been fucking through it."

"Gen, that's not helpful," Tati admonishes her. "You were dehydrated, and I think whatever mode of transportation that AI managed really does a number on humans. Your final episode was two weeks ago."

"Two weeks?" I croak, not quite believing it. "I've been unconscious for two weeks?"

"No, two weeks was how long the interstellar transference lasted," Gen answers. "We really need a better name for that."

"Two weeks," I repeat again, shocked. "Has anyone else made it here? Are my friends okay?"

"They're still being streamed. We've made contact with the AI in an attempt to barter for their release, but it's not interested." This comes from a tall dark green Suevan, thick black hair falling over his shoulders. "We do not understand what it wants."

"We are working on it," a beautiful brunette at his side chimes in, and I glance down, noticing a tail wrapped around her calf. "The important thing is that you are safe, and though your friends appear to be in danger, the AI is keeping true to the contract you signed."

The doctor, Tati, runs a wand over my body. "Your vitals are good. Nothing some more vitamins and fluids won't set right. That and some sleep."

"Do you want to see your new house? Abby has been working like a wild thing to make sure everything is set up at the colony." Gen grins at me. A little green-skinned blonde toddler races into the room, giggling. She's the spitting image of Gen, albeit a green version, and the woman scoops her up and kisses her forehead. "We're all excited to show you."

"Cited," the little girl croons, waving a chubby hand at me.

"Yeah," I say softly, squeezing Rex's hand. "I want to see where we'll be living."

"You don't have to live with him if you don't want to," Gen says hurriedly, and Tati nods. "We have a women's quarters you are welcome to stay in if you prefer your own space. We both lived there for a while, it's a nice myza."

"Myza?" I repeat, mystified.

"It's like a luxury tree house," the black-haired woman explains. "I'm Niki, by the way. We know that you two mated, but we're not like the Draegon or the Arco or even the Roth—we won't force either of you to stay together if you don't want to, okay?"

Rex is silent. He's been silent this whole time, just holding me.

I realize with a start he's waiting for me to make up my mind. He's quiet because he wants it to be my decision.

My heart aches with happiness.

"I want to stay with Ka-Rexsh," I say quietly, looking up at him and only at him.

"Forever?" Gen asks, and Niki elbows her.

"Not nice," the blonde toddler scolds Niki.

"We'll see," I tell her, and then I kiss Ka-Rexsh. "For now, at least."

"I can work with this for now," he says, beaming down at me.

"I love you," I tell him. "Let's go see what we've won."

"Well, some of it got beamed in with you. There's a comms tablet, and it looks like you can communicate with the women still in the game, though I couldn't hack into it, for whatever reason." A tiny muscular woman is sitting on the floor with stuff piled all around her. "I'm Bex. I do tech. And my husband." She lets out a feral cackle. "And I might have to order some of this shit for myself because it is right up my alley."

"Of course you want to," Gen says loudly, rolling her eyes.

"Oh, come on, look, who doesn't want this?" she holds up a pink blanket patterned in pastels. "This one says 'monster fucker.' This other one says 'we cum in peace.'" She points to the design.

I blink. "Okay, I hate to be a killjoy, but I have no idea what is going on right now and I kind of want to be alone with Rex."

"So you can come in peace?" the one called Bex asks, giving an exaggerated wink.

"Bex," Tati groans.

I get the distinct feeling that Bex is like this all the time.

"I saw on the show you like alien fanfic," Bex continues like nothing's happened.

"I'd rather find my own alien happy ending," I tell her, winking.

"I will give you your happy ending," Rex tells me, then pulls me into his chest, giving me another kiss.

"Yeah you will," Bex says, and I laugh a little, relief at my reality TV stint being over warring with my fear for my friends.

"Take me to our new home," I tell Rex.

So he does just that.

As for real-life happy endings, I find that I'm definitely even more a fan of those than I am of any on reality TV.

EPILOGUE

LILY

Zan is pissing me off.

Not that there's anything unusual about that. The huge purple Draegon seems to know exactly how to push my buttons, and what's worse, he delights in doing it.

Right now, pushing my buttons consists of singing, off-key, the alien version of ninety-nine bottles of beer on the wall.

It is, as it turns out, the actual song that never ends.

"Can you knock it the fuck off?" I ask.

We're going on day three of nothing but the food we can find in this god-forsaken place, and the worst sleep I've ever had in my entire fucking life.

Then there is the heat.

I am, very literally, not a happy camper.

The heat is the worst. I'm sweating constantly, and

despite being the temperature of a volcano, I also have chills. Constantly. Sweating, shivering, shaking—this Draegon-induced heat is not for the faint of heart.

"I will stop singing if you let me mate you," Zan tells me, for the fifteenth time.

This morning, I solved a puzzle that allowed us to have the translators inserted, and I'm wishing I hadn't because this is the constant refrain I get on top of the alien song from hell.

"Leave me the fuck alone," I growl. "I'd rather stick my wet hair into an electrical socket than let you stick your plug into me."

Zan lets out a rip-roaring laugh, as if we're old buddies and I've just made the best joke he's ever heard.

"You don't want me to leave," he says, staring at me. "You won't survive on your own."

"Fuck you."

"That is the general idea, yes." He nods, eyes gleaming.

I hate—hate—that the way he says it, that syrupy, sensual voice paired with his gorgeous alien face and perfect, tall body, makes me wet.

And it's all his fault because he poisoned me with his stupid-ass mating serum, which is making me both horny and miserable.

"It is a figure of SPEECH!" I scream. "GO AWAY."

He blinks.

His wings fan out, and without another word, the white-haired purple Draegon sails off into the sky.

Slightly stunned, I watch him disappear, spiraling higher and higher, until he's a speck in the sky.

Finally. Silence.

I let out a sigh, relieved and yet totally worried to be on my own, and then continue on the blatant path the damned AI made for us. I'm sure Zan will be back, but until he is, I'm going to enjoy the peace and quiet.

My mood improves every second he's gone, so much so that I'm humming to myself and walking briskly along the path, hardly paying attention to where I am, just happy not to listen to Zan beg for sex or sing that torturous song anymore.

I don't see the trap until it's too late.

Which is why, I suppose, it's a trap—because you don't see it. That's the whole point.

The noose tightens around my ankle, and then I'm hauled into the air, hanging by my right leg, which very quickly starts to lose sensation as I swing around.

"Help." I cry out, hoping, for the first time, that Zan will come running.

He doesn't come running.

He doesn't come flying.

"Help," I yell again, flailing around, trying to get loose, and only succeeding in spinning around like fishing bait.

Thinking the word bait makes me fall silent.

Bait is not something I want to compare myself too, and I think it might be all too close to reality.

Dark is starting to fall by the time I hear something crashing through the underbrush. I'm barely conscious, thanks to hanging upside down for god only knows how long.

"Zan," I say weakly. "I'm so sorry; I was wrong, please cut me down, I need you."

I scream as I come face-to-face with the thing that was crunching through the forest.

It's not Zan, and this isn't good. Not good at all.

AFTERWORD: A NOTE FROM JANUARY

If you enjoyed this book, it would mean the world to me if you left a review!

Thank you, readers, for joining me on this absurd and silly adventurous alien romance! It's been so much fun to be back in this world, and I hope you're as excited as I was to see some familiar characters.

I'll be continuing this series with Zan and Lily's book, likely in just a few months, if everything goes according to plan! Juggling two pen names this year and publishing contracts has slowed me down significantly, but I hope to be back to my quicker pace soon.

I owe all of you a huge thank you for continuing to spread the word about my books and cheer me on, SO THANK YOU!

If you haven't checked it out yet, I have very pretty special editions, signed paperbacks, and merchandise on my site, www.januarybellromance.com , and it's definitely worth a look!

ALSO BY JANUARY BELL

FANTASY TITLES:

WILD OAK WOODS WORLD:

How To Tame A Trickster Fae

How To Woo A Warrior Orc

How To Please A Princely Fae

A CONQUEROR'S KINGDOM

Of Sword & Silver

Of Gods & Gold

FATED BY STARLIGHT

Following Fate: Prequel Novella

Claimed By The Lion: Book One

Stolen By The Scorpio: Book Two

Taurus Untamed: Book Three

SCIENCE FICTION TITLES:

MATED & AFRAID

Alien Jeopardy

Alien Survivor

ACCIDENTAL ALIEN BRIDES

Wed To The Alien Warlord

Wed To The Alien Prince

Wed To The Alien Brute

Wed To The Alien Gladiator

Wed To The Alien Beast

Wed To The Alien Assassin

Wed To The Alien Hunter

Wed To The Alien Rogue

BOUND BY FIRE

Alien On Fire

Alien in Flames

ALIEN DATING GAMES

Alien Tides

ABOUT THE AUTHOR

January Bell writes steamy fantasy and sci-fi romance with a guaranteed happily ever after. Combining pure escapism, a little adventure, and a whole lotta love makes for romance that's a world apart. January spends her days writing, herding kids and ducks, and spends the nights staring at the stars.

For the latest updates, sign up for my newsletter by visiting www.januarybellromance.com, or follow me on Instagram and TikTok.

Printed in Dunstable, United Kingdom